SPARKS
OF THE
MOUNTAIN

Book One

JORDAN BATT

PAGE PUBLISHING
Conneaut Lake, PA

First originally published by Page Publishing 2023

ISBN 979-8-88960-336-8 (pbk)
ISBN 979-8-88960-348-1 (digital)

Printed in the United States of America

CHAPTER 1

W HEN YOU END UP doing the same things all the time, the routine becomes comfortable. Before you even know it, you're in a slump that got there all on its own. Life just happens so naturally like the flow of the river. You wake up every morning and make a cup of coffee, take a shower, and go about your day like always. Doing chores is the highlight of your time before settling down for the night.

My life had that kind of routine, though it was still filled with daydreams and wishes. I had a nice quiet life. When I moved out of the pack house at eighteen and into my own place on the edge of the pack lands, I just wanted the peace of the lands around me. It seemed like it was a safe place to settle down and maybe someday fall in love. Though as time went on, love wasn't something I wanted to look for. I'm content with the simplicity of the way I live. I may not have the kind of life everyone seems appropriate for an alpha's daughter.

That is the bright side about being the youngest and better behaved of two daughters though. I seem to be able to slip under the radar by choice. With the way my other sister goes about being, well, herself, I'm simple and like to just curl up with a nice book with some tea. Not with some random guy who doesn't have a clue what a proper conversation is. To grab my sister's attention, all you have to do is be a *Neanderthal* that couldn't even rub two sticks together if he has too. Though because of this I was able to discreetly move out of the pack house. One night when a *Neanderthal* got caught trying to sneak into the house, I got out during the commotion without even being noticed until the next morning. It felt amazing to be away from

1

the noise in a small cabin that was left to me. It is tucked quietly away in the woods, right at the edge of our pack's land. I was surrounded by trees with birds singing. I swear even the air here smells different than anywhere else I've ever been. It is somewhere I could work on my writing and live in peace without many distractions.

It is a nice little cabin that is surrounded by beautiful trees. My favorite spot is the front porch. I have a rocking chair out there under the roof where I can sit and watch the rain fall. It is easy to get lost in your thoughts when you are sitting out there. The peace that comes over you is something I could never give up. The trees blew in the wind, making creaking sounds. It is like the trees are talking to each other as the branches are swaying left and right in harmony. I spend most of my nights out there no matter what the weather is like, just to watch the open nature, unwinding from all the conversations and brainwork of the day.

That was where I was when I saw the first signs of trouble starting in the mountains past our land markings. The light show that started up was something that would be talked about for years to come with shock and awe. When the pack children asked where I was when history was made, this was my answer: sitting on the porch only to see colors start to light up in the clouds. The colors were not natural and brought me to my feet to look over the railing. They were flashing in frantic motion in the clouds. Reds, greens, and blue lightning bolts that looked like the bolts were attacking each other up in the clouds. It was so unnatural that I couldn't even help but just stare at the show.

This was going to be known as the night the witches of the East decided to attack. No one knew it was coming; they hadn't given us any warning. Though the only thing I could think of that could make lightning like that is witches. That wasn't the kind of magic that we practiced. Magic use of nature should be natural for the environment. There was nothing natural about the colors of those bolts of lightning or the awful screeching noise that was coming from high in the mountains. The bangs shook the trees and ground so violently that I wondered if that was what an earthquake felt like. I had never felt an earthquake before, though if it felt like that, I knew I didn't want to feel it. The ground was shaking so hard that it felt the moon goddess herself picked the earth up and was shaking some sense into it.

I moved to get a better look up into the night sky that was filled with rays of colors. The colors were flying up in all directions, and every time the light streaks hit the sky, they crackled like thunder. Reds, blues, and greens shooting up with sparks. Smoke was coming from the treetops. It was almost floating like a large black cloud and started to drift toward our lands. The trees started to move, almost blowing over and bending till the tops of some looked like they were going to touch the ground, bowing away from the mountain like they wished they could pick up their roots and run away from whatever was going on up there. The noise was frightening and something I had never heard before nor do I wish to ever hear again. It was almost indescribable, the deafening drums of an unseeable battle shaking the ground under my feet. I stood frozen in place, watching the mountains scream and cry in battle.

The mountains were thought to be untouchable. The strongest of all the packs are known to reside up there. They are believed to be the true descendants of the Old Ones, the original wolves known as the Lucan. Their main job among the packs is to be the peacekeepers of the lands, only coming down from the mountains when called into a battle if they choose to. They hold no allegiance with any packs or anyone for that matter. They are the boogeymen packs told their cubs about to make them behave or "the mountain will come down to get you." It is believed and told throughout generations that the mountains are not somewhere we want to go. It isn't land that you would want to visit. The stories that were told over so many generations killed any curiosity the mountains would give most people. A healthy fear comes over you when you would venture too far up the hills, doing groundwork or hunting. It is a feeling like you are being watched, but you never see anything when you look around. An instinct deep inside tells you to turn around and not to look back. Only the insane or demented would ignore these feelings.

This would be the night that went down in our people's history. As the night the mountains lit up, sending a wave of terror falling down to the lands below, I couldn't think of a single person who would be dumb enough to try and fight the mountains. Though as I watched, it was clear something very bad was happening high above the trees. You could feel the earth rumbling in rage.

As I watched the skies light up in anger, I could hear the howling screams. They sounded like they were coming closer. Something was very wrong, and the feeling made me move away from the safety of my cabin porch and go further and further into the woods. I didn't know what was pulling me closer to the petrifying sounds, but I couldn't stop my feet from moving. Before I knew what was happening, I shifted into my wolf on instinct and was running up the hills and cliffs on my four paws as fast as I could. I knew it wasn't smart, but I needed to get up there because something up there was drawing me with a force that was unexplainable. As I ran, boulders were flying overhead, causing me to dodge and weave through the small bushes and baby trees. The boulders were large, some probably as wide as my arms' length in human form. I refused to think about what could be strong enough to throw them through the air. The thought would probably have me turn around and hightail it out of there as if the hounds of darkness were after me, though my adrenaline was racing too hard to think clearly.

Instead I barreled forward until I heard the crying clearer. As I got closer, the crying sounds were growing stronger until I came across some pups hidden behind a large fallen tree trunk. They were two little boys; they could only be about five or six years old. One of the boys was kneeling, and he had to be just a little bit older than the one laying on the ground. I was only about a mile away from my little cabin. As I came closer, I could see the fallen tree that was on the boy's leg as he was crying in pain and fear. The other boy was trying to calm him while pulling on his leg to free it. The trunk wouldn't budge because it was pinned down between the ground and a boulder.

I shifted back into my human self once I got close enough to the boys to crouch down. "It's okay, babies, it's okay. Here, let me help you."

I went up to the boulder and started to push with all my strength, relieved there was a little hill going downward behind it so gravity

4

could help until the boulder gave way. The boulder rolled down the hill and crashed into the ground with a massive smashing sound. The trunk was large, and I didn't know where I got the strength to lift it, but I put my arms under the trunk around the boy's leg and pulled up as hard as I could. It had to be the adrenaline coursing through my veins, managing to lift it just high enough for the oldest boy to pull his friend out. And he held him as they both cried.

I turned around and scooped the injured boy up. "Come on, follow me." I turned with the hurt boy and started back down the mountain toward my cabin. Turning around only to check to see if the older boy was following, and he was right on my heels running his heart out all the way back to the cabin.

"Okay, let's take a look at that leg, huh?"

I ran into the bathroom to grab my first aid box and rushed back to the couch. It looked broken and had a big bloody gash carved into his shin. I knew with the sounds of the battle so close that there was nothing I could really do for him, so I did my best to wrap and set the leg. I wrapped the gash up and did my best to create a make-shift brace. Thankful for the basic medical training I had, so I at least had an idea of what to do for him. When this was all over, I was going to have to talk to my friend, Bonnie, for more training.

Once that was taken care of, I covered the boys up with a blanket and turned to the other boy. "Stay here and look after him. I'll be right back. I'm going to go see if there is anyone else out there that needs help. Everything is going to be fine, okay? Stay here."

And with that, I took up for the mountain again and again, finding women and children with each trip, taking them back down to the flatlands. Every trip I took up the mountain took me higher and higher until the bangs and booms of the witches' magical explosions made my ears ring, and I started gathering up the injured warriors that had fallen at the sudden battle land that used to be the Great Mountains. Changing back and forth from into my wolf form was exhausting, but every time I started to feel the drain to my body, another explosion went off, causing more adrenaline to course through me. It was pushing my wolf forward.

It was like the earth around me was on fire. The winds were screeching around me as the earth shook with each bolt of lightning slamming into it with an unimaginable force. One of the lightning bolts landed just off to my left side. The force of it threw my wolf into a tree, though I ignored the pain in my body. The rage running through my wolf form got me back to my feet as I pushed myself closer to the fight. The howls of the hurt wolves that were fighting a force that you couldn't even see moved around you. I saw a group of she-wolves that had formed a circle around some pups, ready to defend them from the witch that was moving closer to them. Their teeth were bared, snarling in warning. I turned toward them, charging forward. As I got closer, I noticed the witch had an odd look in her eyes. There was no white in them; they were completely black.

I slammed into the back of the witch and bit down hard. Using my claws and my back legs to kick out. Ripping into her back and bringing her to the ground. The taste in my mouth from the hold I had on her was wrong. She didn't taste of blood or earth. Instead it was more like an oily slime. Though now wasn't the time for thinking. Once the witch stopped moving, I let go of her. I looked over at the other she-wolves to find them gathering the pups around, getting ready to make a run for it. They were staring at me with an unease that came with the moment of horror that was all around them. I must have looked a sight up there. I was an unknown she-wolf covered in mud and blood on my fur as leaves were stuck to me. I nodded my head at them then swung toward the direction I came from. I turned and ran toward the hurt wolves not looking to see if they took my cue.

It wasn't until I started gathering the injured wolves that I knew some of the women must have made it down to the flatlands because men from my pack started to come up. The whole time trying to stay away from the fires and flashes of bright lights. After a few trips up and down the mountain, it started becoming quieter. Though the silence was worse than the screams in a way because it was just eerie. You didn't even hear the night owls or the mockingbirds that sang their songs until late into the night. Just a wall of silence all around me.

By the time all the warriors had assembled and gotten there, I was so tired and sore. I sat on the ground outside of the pack hospital and was looking at the grounds that were covered in injured wolves. I couldn't even tell you how many trips I made that night. Though it was a heartbreaking scene to see the destruction that lay all around me, I may not know these people. But no one deserves such violence.

Once I got my breath back, I went into the hospital to see if they needed anything from me before I went home. I didn't want to leave without checking just to make sure they didn't need any help. Goddess Bless Eager who was a gruff elder of the pack met me outside the hospital door, carrying a pair of scrubs. Without a word, he handed me the scrubs, turning me around by the shoulders, and sent me on my way. He wasn't one for many words, but it was clear that that night, he truly was at a complete loss for them. But I got to the point that there was nothing more I could do there. Looking around me, I could feel my eyes start to sting with tears that I couldn't let fall yet.

The air around the grounds had this dark cloud of mist laying all around it. It felt like you were standing in a humidifier; the fog was becoming so think. The atmosphere had changed, and the moon goddess started to cry. The rain that started to fall was getting heavier by the minute. I made my way back to my once quiet cabin only to find that it was empty with a note on my coffee table from a woman in town. The note was letting me know they came and got the boys at some point in the night. That was good because they needed proper medical care. I was feeling completely absolutely drained of energy. Nothing seemed right.

Once I got inside the threshold, the events of the night seemed almost surreal. The fact that I ran up that mountain and all the devastation I saw scattered around the ground. The noises and blood were everywhere. It was unimaginable, everything that I had seen. Shutting the door, my muscles finally went out, and I laid back on the door taking in a few deep breaths to bring what strength I had left to the surface, so I could make my way to the bathroom and run a tub. A tub sounded nice; that and a good cup of calming tea should make me feel more like myself. More like the calming I liked and needed in my life. With the tub running and the teapot heating on the gas stove, I sat at my table and listened to the nothingness that was now coming from outside. Hard to believe that just a few hours ago, screams of battle were coming from the skies that were never seen before, and now there was just the eerie silence and banging of rain that didn't seem to be stopping anytime soon.

With the whistle raging from the tea kettle begging to be taken off the stove top, I grabbed it and made the much-needed cup to calm my shot nerves and went to soak in the tub. Wishing to just wash away the memories of the reverberating booms and screams from the night. Hoping desperately that the feelings of the need to run away would pass. Once in the bathroom, I stripped out of the hospital scrubs they gave me to cover up my nakedness from all the shifting back and forth. One step into the tub had my knees shaking and buckling as the shock of what just happened really started to kick in. I slid down to sit, pulling my knees up to my chest to rest my head on them, and started to cry. After a few more breaths to calm my nerves, I started to wash the grime off. I looked down at myself and saw all the bruises that started to form. Luckily, they would fade in a day or two. Leaning back and sipping the tea until I felt completely calm enough where I could trust my legs to carry me out of the bathroom, I got out of the tub, dried off being extra gentle at the darkest bruises. I had no idea the exact moment I got them. I slipped on my pajamas and made my way to my bedroom.

When I got into the bedroom, I looked out the window and could see the sun starting to rise. An orange glow was just starting to shine through the trees. I found it odd that after such a horrendous night that the morning after could have such a pretty glow. The hue of the orange and pink were truly something to behold. I made my way to the window to close the curtain and then fell into bed, cocooning myself in the blankets. Glancing at the clock, I found that it was a little after six thirty in the morning. As I lay there, I realized I was holding my breath as panic started to come back. I took another deep breath when I felt my heart start to accelerate again. Lying there until exhaustion finally began to take over my body, I drifted off to a surprisingly deep dreamless sleep. The only thought was to have this bad dream be over with when I wake.

CHAPTER 2

WAKING UP AND FEELING like I was run over by a truck was not something I thought of as fun. My legs felt like they were jelly and on fire, and when I turned over to stretch, something pulled in my back. I couldn't give it much thought though because when I turned over, I came face-to-face with one of the boys from last night. He was sitting cross-legged and was staring at me with a big smile on his face.

"Umm, good morning," I said, tipping my head slightly to the side to get a better look at him.

"Mornin'. You're a really heavy sleeper," the boy said and then he just sat there.

So I just went to get up, sliding on my bunny slippers. I found they'll but wonder what the kid was doing back here so early.

"With all the excitement last night, a deep sleep was needed," I said with a small laugh and started to make my way to the kitchen.

Coffee was definitely going to be needed before starting this day. I grabbed my coffee pot to fill with water and slid the kitchen window open almost simultaneously. I took in a deep breath of air. The fresh air was cold and crisp that blew in right away, raising the curtains into the air. The wildflowers I clipped the other day were swirling around in the crystal-blue glass vase. It was coming from the south, away from the mountains that was to the north of my back door. I turned with the pot of water and almost bumped into the kid 'cause he was standing right behind my leg, watching what I was doing. In the light of day, after all the excitement passed, I finally got a good look at him. He had sandy-blond hair and the greenest eyes I'd ever seen. They reminded me of grass after a heavy rainfall.

"What's up, honey? You want something to eat or something?" I asked, thinking he had to be hungry.

He looked so small to me for a wolf pup and breakfast didn't sound like a bad idea.

"Alpha's coming, aren't you going to get ready?" He seemed both excited and exasperated at the same time. Almost bouncing in his spot as he spoke.

"Sweetie, I won't be meeting your alpha." With a shake of my head, I poured the water into the pot to make the liquid of the gods.

"Why not?" He was still bouncing.

He kind of reminded me of an energizer bunny. Something about him reminded me of a big ball of energy. I think it was his green eyes. As he bounced, his eyes had a twinkle to them that almost looked like gold flecks.

"The alphas have a lot to go over and have to talk about everything that happened last night. I would just get in the way at that kind of meeting. The war room is no place for me, sweetie. And I think your alpha came last night, a little after four when the rains started. An Alpha William, right?"

The boy, to her shock, busted out laughing. He was laughing so hard he bent over, holding onto his stomach. Whatever was so funny I didn't know, but as the boy cackled, I went to pour myself a cup of coffee. Yes, coffee was going to be needed, especially if this was any indication of what the day was going to be like. I made my way into the living room only to stop and see two other children sitting on the couch. These boys were older than the one that was now my shadow, who was still giggling like a lune as he continued to follow behind me.

"That's not our alpha," one of the new boys said, clearly hearing our conversation all the way from the kitchen, and he too started to laugh.

If I had to guess, I would say he was the oldest of the three. He had black hair with caramel-brown eyes. He seemed to be the one in charge of the group of boys that clearly have settled into my living room. I looked around the living room, and it had blankets over the couch with pillows from my spare room. There was an empty bag of chips and water bottles sitting on the coffee table. A part of me was happy they had just made themselves at home, though I was confused as to how I ended up with three children that I didn't know were squatting in my living room. I was pretty sure they weren't there when I got home last night.

When the oldest boy stood from my couch, grabbing my attention from looking around the room, he held his head up high. Though he looked off to my left not meeting my eyes, it was a sign of respect, but I found it odd coming from someone that was still so young. The mountains were thought to be different, though maybe this was just one of the differences from how their children are raised versus ours. From what I understood, the mountains were like a completely different culture. Which made sense considering the reputation it held. Though the pride the boy stood with shocked me slightly, it was clear he would be an alpha one day when he grew into his teeth. What kind of alpha wasn't quite clear yet.

"Well, let's get some food into you boys and go from there. Growing wolves have to eat, right?" I turned back on my heels and made my way back into the kitchen. Though now instead of having one shadow, I now had three.

"Well, sit down and let's see what we have." Rummaging through my fridge, I came up with eggs and bread.

Throwing them on the counter, I grabbed a frying pan and got to work on a quick meal while the children watched me. The eldest boy was standing in the doorway with his back against the door-frame. He was just watching everything around him. I didn't miss the way his eyes moved through the room, and I knew he was watching for any threat or attack. The thought that a child would feel the need to watch so carefully for something to happen broke my heart. Children should just be playing and not have to worry about such things. Though he gave me a feeling he hasn't played for a long time, he seemed content to be guarding the room rather than joining the boys at the table. I figured it would be best not to push him.

"When did you boys get here? Where did you boys hide during the fighting? You're going to need a bath. If you wish, you are welcome to shower here after you eat something," I said, trying to break the silence and get them to open up a little bit.

They were different from the children of my pack. Normally, the boys from around here talked and wrestled nonstop. These boys weren't saying much of anything, and they didn't make a move to answer my questions.

So I figured I would try a different line of questioning. "Who is your alpha if it isn't Alpha William? Do you need help finding your pack?"

"You ask a lot of questions," the one in the doorway said, shocking me enough to look over my shoulder at him only to find him staring straight at me, looking me right in the eyes.

He was showing a great disrespect and was trying to challenge me. Something I found off because he wasn't yet of the age to challenge adults. Normally when the pups start challenging, they challenge other boys and some of the younger men around them. It's our way of finding our ranks in the pack life. Not the women. The look in his eyes was unnerving, especially considering it was coming from a child. Well, that wasn't going to work for me. It was too early to deal with a little pup with an attitude no matter what was going on in the world. It was best to deal with these moments head-on if you were to ask me. So I squared my shoulders and handled the pup just like I would if he were mine. Since this was my home, it seemed appropriate.

"Yes and questions that I expect an answer to, little one." I turned fully from the counter and matched the boy's stare with one of my own. Slowly, I moved away from the stove and took a few steps toward him with my hands on my hips.

"Our alpha is Alpha Damien, the Rapture," said the young boy from the other night, my little shadow of the morning.

Clearly, he was trying to break the tension away from the one that was giving me the attitude. I knew deep down the oldest was just testing me, but if he was going to be in my house, he needed to know my rules straight off the bat. I had a good feeling if I let him, he would take over the house. I didn't think he would be one to give back power once he got it.

"We're from his pack. It's higher up the mountain than Alpha William's is. It's smaller than his, too, but stronger. They are the ones that come down to help fight or train the packs down here." There was a lot of pride said with the last bit.

"Tommy," said the boy moving off the doorframe to stand to his full height in a clear warning.

I wasn't sure where he was taking intimidation lessons, but those classes were not going to be practiced in my cabin. It was obvious he didn't need any practice.

"Why don't you just sit down and join your friends," I said, walking up behind him and dropping my hand on his shoulder to steer him toward the chair. It was a dominant move, but there were going to be rules if they were going to be in my home.

This was going to be a long day. The moon goddess knew that I didn't have enough coffee yet on this glorious morning to be dealing with three youngsters I seemed to have taken in at some point while I slept. How that worked, I didn't know, but I was okay with it.

"When did you boys get down here? Where did you stay last night?" I asked them.

"They came after the fighting had stopped," the boy whose name was apparently Tommy said as he drank some juice he helped himself to from the fridge.

"Why did you wait so long to come? You weren't hurt, were you?" I moved away from the stove again, the breakfast almost done, to look the boys over making sure there were no injuries on them.

"We were helping move the women out of the lands down the mountain. Our alpha wasn't there to charge into battle," this came from the alpha in the making.

"That's why the witches won last night. If our alpha was there, they wouldn't have stood a chance. He would have charged his way right through all of them. When he gets back, he'll get the mountains back and under control," the other boy that was sitting quietly the whole time said.

13

"The witches looked weird. They had on these black robes and were chanting and waving their arms around. This one witch was pointing into the sky and lightning started coming from wherever she pointed. Though the lightning didn't look natural. It was bright colors and fell down in random directions. A few times, I thought it was going to hit the witches that were with her. It was like it went wherever it felt like. They moved in a line toward us. Big rocks started flying through the air. They hit some of the houses, going into them."

"Yeah, when I was coming down here, there were trees down everywhere and little fires going in the woods. I put some of the fires out as I went but then it started to rain, so I just started running. I followed some of the fighters I saw making their way back here," said the alpha-to-be.

"You boys must have been scared. Everything will be okay now. We will figure out what to do, and everything will go back to normal. I promise you boys that. You do sound very proud of your alpha, though. He must be a brave man," I said. "So you're Tommy"—I nodded to the youngest—"it's very nice to meet you, young man. And what's your name, hun?" asked the quiet boy with a smile on his face.

"I'm Danny, and the ass over there is Manny. We're brothers. Our uncle is Alpha William, though we live with Damien. We are in training to be warriors. Manny over there thinks he is going to have what it takes to be alpha," Danny said as he crossed his arms.

"Well, it's always good to have goals. My name is Isabel, and it's nice to meet you, boys," I said as I served the pancakes, eggs, and toast.

Not wanting to admit I thought the same thing about Manny being an alpha one day, the boy's head seemed to be big enough already, and I didn't want him running off and doing something he wasn't ready for. I had a good idea that if the thought struck the boy, Manny, he would go right up there himself to see the witches. I could see the want swimming in his eyes as he kept glancing at the door. His agitation was understandable, but this wasn't the time for him to prove himself. This was a time for him to watch and learn. I was going to have to be creative in distracting him somehow.

Once the food was served to the boys, they ate with gusto. You would think they hadn't eaten in days with the way they attacked the food. Not a table manner to be seen but it was almost kind of endearing the way they forgot to chew. Talking around bites about every and anything, the morning mood was eased as they ate. You know what they say, the way to a man's heart is through their stomachs. The same thing clearly could be said for the three boys sitting at my table because they all seemed to relax when they were eating their fill.

"Tommy, is your friend okay from last night?" I asked, remembering the other child that was with him.

"Yeah, he's going to be fine. I had to leave him with the nurse lady though. She wouldn't let me take him."

"I'm sorry, honey. I'm sure he's in good hands though. We have very good nurses here."

"You patched his leg up last night though, so why can't you take care of him?" Tommy asked shining those big green eyes up at me.

"I only know basic first aid, and I learned it from my best friend who happens to be one of the nurses watching after. She knows a lot more than I do, and I promise he's going to be taken good care of. He's probably getting spoiled right now."

"Spoiled? We're the ones that got pancakes." This came from Danny.

"Yeah, normally we only get pancakes if it's a special occasion, like our birthdays or a holiday or something like that," Manny said, coming around for the sugary goodness that was the syrup.

"Really? What do you guys normally eat for breakfast then?"

"Eggs, cereal, toast. Mostly whatever we gather during the hunts or what comes back on the trucks when Doc gets back from the towns."

"Who's Doc?" I laughed.

"Doc is Alpha Damien's second. He goes to town every other month and buys supplies," Manny said. "I got to go with him last month. We filled the back of the pickup truck. There was even stuff in the back seats."

As I was cleaning up the mess of the kitchen, I froze when the talking at the table fell silent. I turned around to find Wayne standing at my kitchen table, apparently letting himself in without knocking. The boys had moved to the doorway and were glaring at the man. I had never really liked Wayne. He always reminded me more of a weasel or a small dog than a wolf. Thankfully though, I never really had to deal with him. Why he would feel comfortable enough to just walk into my home, I didn't know. The only guess I could come up with was the fact that he used to see my sister. Still does on and off probably considering Stacy likes to keep her options open.

He is always whining and going on about something. I never paid him any attention nor he me, and I liked it that way. He always gave me the creeps that made my skin crawl. It was a good sign that I just didn't want to get too close to him. He had a silver tongue that always seemed to get him what he wanted. He had the ability to be able to talk his way into any situation he wanted to be in. He had a gift of being able to manipulate a moment to his advantage. If I was to guess by the glares Manny and Danny had on their faces, I would think they both instinctively felt the same thing. Especially given the fact that they moved little Tommy behind them in a protective gesture. The instinct was strong in these boys.

Some part of me wanted Wayne to go over by them simply for the fact that I wanted to see what the boys would do. The curiosity about what would happen didn't matter because I wasn't really in the mood for whatever game Wayne had in mind this morning. He was always more of a pretty boy. His brown hair was perfectly combed to the side, and he always wore some nice sweater coat with a name brand patched on it. He wanted to look the part of someone important but always fell just off the mark. He always looked completely put together. Though to be fair Wayne never did anything wrong, I was just going off a feeling he gave me. He was more of the puppet master than a player in the game of life we had here. It was a game that I, unlike my sister, stayed away from. Growing up, I was taught that if you didn't understand the rules of the game, you shouldn't play. It would only be a good way to lose whatever it was that you were playing for.

"What are you doing in here?" I said, putting my hand on my hip.

"I just wanted to check in on you after all the excitement from last night. I thought maybe you would be scared and needed a friend to lean on," he said as he made his way around the table.

I locked my knees in place to hold my ground, having no intention to back down in my own kitchen. I was too tired to really care about anything he had to say.

Seriously, I was going to have to start locking the door if this was what I had to look forward to in my future. Pop and stops weren't on my happy-go-lucky list and not something I wanted to be thought of as welcomed. It kind of defeated the point of moving to the edge of the pack grounds when you get uninvited guests. The funny thing was I never wished I locked my door before this visit.

"Well, thank you for checking but my nerves have held up just fine. Thank you," I said, putting my chin out and holding my head high.

Though I could faintly hear one of the boys start to growl from the doorway, instinct told me not to look away from the male that was now arm's reach from me to turn and see which one it was.

"Thank you for stopping by, Wayne, but if you could please excuse me, I have my hands full this morning." Raising my hand, I gestured to the door. A gesture that went completely ignored as the arrogance flowed out of Wayne in waves.

"Yes, I see that. Where did you get the little ones from?" Wayne asked, looking behind me, at the boys standing in the doorway.

At least I thought they were still in the doorway until I felt movement from right behind my legs. I didn't glance down to see which of the boys had come forward. For the little time I had spent with them, I had a good feeling it was Manny. He didn't seem too shy to hide from strangers. And I was right, Manny was standing at my legs with a really unhappy look on his face.

"Oh, from here and there." I laughed, reaching behind me to try shooing the boy back to the doorway to stand with the others.

He didn't move away though, and I can't explain the feeling I had in my stomach, but I didn't really want the kids close at the moment. There was a look to Wayne that really just wasn't sitting well with me. Call it instinct or paranoia, but something said to move the children away. Though my brain told me I was being nuts and that Wayne wasn't going to hurt them, my stomach still said something else. It was a motherly feeling. It was an odd experience to have. Never really having to spend time with him, I didn't know where this overprotective feeling was coming from.

"Very vague Isabel." He laughed and moved to sit at the table, clearly not planning on leaving anytime soon, so I just poured another cup of coffee and kept my face polite like a good hostess.

"I'm not too sure to be honest but they are more than welcome to stay in my cabin. Especially with everything going on. I'm happy to take them in."

"Yes, that had to be a terrible fright for you. I'm here if you ever want to talk about it. It's good to know you have a motherly nature. When you have pups of your own, that will be important. Especially if you want to breed strong ones," Wayne said, reaching over the table and taking hold of my hand.

I tried to tug away gracefully, but he didn't let go. It wasn't until Manny was standing at the table, growling like a caged animal, that I realized my struggling was noticeable to the children, defeating my attempt not to scare the kids any more than they were, that are now apparently in my care. So I just ripped my hand away and reached down to settle a very unhappy Manny.

"Yes. The night's events are something to be discussed. Though I'm thinking that you may not be the one she wishes to talk to about them. Guessing from the warm welcome you're receiving," came a deep male voice from behind me near the children.

I jumped to my feet not hearing someone else enter my home that was turning into grand central station. I couldn't really think of a time I had so much traffic in my little home.

There in the doorway standing behind Tommy and Danny stood a tall broad man with charcoal-black hair and equally dark eyes. He had an angry scar running down his chin and neck going down the center of his throat. I looked up into the stranger's eyes, so I did not stare at the scar, not wanting to be rude to the uninvited company, especially since I had never met him before. It was a very rough-looking scar with jagged edges. No part of me wanted to think about how he came to get it. Though what I saw in his eyes instead made it almost impossible to look away. Deep down, I knew I needed to look away from his eyes. Nothing good could come from staring at him. They were hard and cold, almost like an unforgiving black hole that you could drown in and never come back from.

Wayne jumped to his feet, snarling like the idiot he was. "Who the hell are you, and what gives you the right to just walk in uninvited?"

I bit the side of my mouth to keep from laughing at the absurdness of the comment he just made considering he walked in without knocking and without invite as well. Though right now was not the right time to laugh at him, with the fact that his face was changing a funny shade of red that didn't look too healthy.

"I'm Alpha Damien and just looking for some lost pups that seemed to have slipped away. And it looks like I found them. Now leave. I have business to discuss." And with that, the newcomer showed Wayne to the door. Literally, he backed Wayne right out the door simply by just walking toward him, making a snarling noise.

At least it answered one of my questions of the morning. I now had a good idea where Manny had taken his intimidation lessons. Wayne backpedaled himself right out the door. The guy that was apparently Damien slammed the door in his face with no care whatsoever then turning back to face the rest of us still in the kitchen. All the boys relaxed when they saw him as if thousands of pounds have been lifted. They all seemed more comfortable than I had seen yet.

I found this whole thing kind of shocking because, well, I didn't like Wayne; at least I knew him. This stranger did not know him or me, and he just came into my home and threw him out. My morning was starting to feel like I entered the twilight zone or an alternate universe. Though the boys seemed completely comfortable with this man. If that was something to go by.

As I was thinking about it, I started to wonder if maybe when I went up the mountain, I did enter an alternate dimension. With all the horror stories about the powers of those hills, it would make sense. Weirder things have been said to happen up in those mountains. Though I didn't feel any different, just very tired. Maybe I can slip away for a nap at some point, and when I get up, life would seem more normal. It couldn't be healthy to try and function on just a few hours of rest. I shook my head to bring my thoughts back to this moment in time. As he turned back around, the boys rushed him, all three of them talking at once, at times yelling over each other to be heard. I listened as they each told the story of everything that happened throughout the night.

I found it rather interesting to listen too. I learned that the boy who had the tree fall on his leg was named Martin and that minus having the cast, he was fine. A part of me felt bad for not asking the boys at the start how he was doing, but at this rate, I wasn't even sure what was happening anymore in my little cabin. The witches had come from all sides of them and was destroying everything in their paths in flashes of colors. Most of the women and children were able to get to the tunnels with the elders of the mountain. The rest stayed to fight or fled down the mountains to the flatlands and got divided apparently. The boys told the whole story of the colors and bangs that shook the lands. The witches came in with flashes of smoke. All the while, Damien sat at the table listening to the full recap, just nodding away until the boys talked themselves out. When the kitchen finally fell silent again, I had all the dishes done, put away, counters washed, and a fresh pot of coffee going. Damien sat there sipping on his cup, thinking over everything that was just babbled over.

When I turned around, he was staring at me with an odd look on his face, sniffing the air like a bloodhound.

"Hi, I'm Isabel," I introduced myself trying to be respectful, though my head was starting to spin.

"Damien" was all he said as he sat there.

Though as I was thinking about everything the boys had said, I did have one question, and since I didn't really know what to say to this alpha, I turned to face the boys with a coffee cup in hand. "I was just wondering how it was you boys came back to my cabin. Wouldn't you have been more comfortable staying with your pack in the heart of the lands instead of here on the edge?"

The answer though left me truly speechless for it came from sweet little Tommy, my morning shadow. "The women were annoying."

"The women were annoying?"

"Yeah, they kept asking if we were okay or if we needed anything. It was weird," Tommy said, nodding like this was a fact that couldn't be disputed.

"So we came here before they woke little before seven because we figured the alpha would come here to talk to you anyway. Since you pulled a lot of his wounded off the mountain." This came from Manny, who gestured with his hand to the alpha that was now sitting at my table.

Damien looked perfectly comfortable to just be sitting at the table. If he was stressed about the events that happened when he was away, you couldn't tell. Though he was still just staring at me.

"And that's why I told you to get ready to meet our alpha," said Tommy who looked me up and down, shaking his head in disappointment. "You didn't listen though."

And that was when I realized that with all the excitement of the morning, I had never gotten dressed for the day and was standing in my kitchen in pajamas with the damn fuzzy bunny slippers looking up at me with those little beanie eyes that I once thought looked so cute but now looked sad after years of being my favorite house shoes. Those sad little droopy ears.

"Oh my..." And on that note, I turned and took off like the hounds of hell were after me for the bedroom, in utter dismay that I could even have sworn the bunnies were even laughing at me.

When I finally came out of the bedroom again, I found the cabin was mostly empty except for Manny, who was sitting on the couch with one of my books.

Before I could say anything though, the little boy looked up at me. "Why don't you have a TV?"

And with that, it was time to just get on with the day.

I made Manny clean up before heading out for the day. I figured a little quality time with him would be good for him to see other ways of doing things. The boy wasn't shy, but I think if I left

21

him to run wild, he would turn the flatlands upside down. Once we were both ready, we headed out, moving down the path toward the town.

Manny wasn't one for random talking, though I did get him to loosen up somewhat when talking about the foods he liked. I pointed out if he didn't tell me what he wanted to eat, he would be stuck with whatever I chose. It was obvious that he didn't wanna leave it to chance that I would actually make something he thought was good. I asked him if he wanted to go to the store with me to help get the stuff we needed.

I realized when he was getting washed up that the boys didn't have any clothes with them. It made the already sad situation they found themselves in more devastating. The fact that the boys had fled their home with nothing besides the clothes on their backs, it made my wolf want to march right up that mountain and have a little talk with the witches myself. My wolf was being very vocal in my head about how much she didn't like the witches' tactics.

Over centuries, our kind has fought with each other and among other kinds, though the children were off limits. I didn't have my head so far in the ground to think that women and children were never affected, but there was a code to fighting. It never should have been like this. Fights like this was why the common laws were even put in place.

CHAPTER 3

MUCH TO MY SURPRISE, the day passed without much more excitement. Manny told me his alpha, the great Alpha Damien, would be coming back to speak with me at another time. He also proclaimed in an alpha-in-the-making tone that the three boys were going to be staying with me until it was time to move on because, and I quote, "don't want to deal with the squawking." I can only assume that he was talking about the women of the pack. Manny, for apparently being only ten years old, didn't have much time to be fond over like a child. No, he was a proud warrior in the making and didn't mind crust on his sandwich, I learned.

To my shock when the boy pointed out the waste of food was to cut off in a perfectly good part of the sandwich, I figured it was best not to argue with him about the current living situation. Mostly because I had a good feeling the boys would just come back. Also, because I thought the women would have a fit getting lectured about food waste from a ten-year-old, of all people. The kid would end up being fed fish stew if I released him to the other women's care. I couldn't let that happen. Instead I took him into town to get groceries. Since I now had three mouths to feed, food was going to be needed. Breakfast was anything to go by when they were hungry and going to eat me out of house and home without much effort if I didn't stock up. Once we reached town, Manny saw the others and took off after them. I figured it would be good for him to run around with the others and just continued on my way to finish the chores of the day. I decided to check in at the hospital to see if they needed anything first. Also, I had to return the scrubs from the night before. So first thing was stopping at the hospital.

Walking into the hospital wasn't what I expected. It was normally filled with friendly greetings and conversations; today it was filled with silence as the people in the beds stopped talking to watch my every move as I went through the room. I recognized some of them from the night before, but I didn't stop to bother any of them. They all looked like they wanted to rest. So keeping my head down, I made my way to the help desk.

"Hey, Bonnie. How are things going in here today?"

"Hey, Izzy. It's been busy. What can I do for you?"

"Nothing. I just wanted to drop this off and see if you needed any help around here. I know you have your hands full."

"Just a little bit." Bonnie laughed.

Bonnie was a sweet girl, always popping on bubble gum and smiling. She was going to make a good doctor one day since she was working her way up to being a pack doctor. Apparently, there was lot of studying that went into it. Sometimes she would come over to the cabin to study. She had to learn human medicine and were-herbs medicine from the current pack doctor. Bonnie even talked to the elders of the lands to help her learn from the storytellers. She believes that knowing the stories of the past can help improve the medicine of the future. The packs historical stories were surprisingly interesting, I have to admit. I liked it when she studied at my place. I always learned something different. Bonnie was honestly my best friend. We were the same age and spent most of our childhood running wild together. Bonnie was always the responsible one of the two of us.

"I think I got everything under control though. Besides, the others will be back soon. They left to get some rest after the crazy night."

"Okay, well, if you need anything, you know where to find me. Oh, and here's the scrubs from last night. Thanks again for letting me borrow them. That would have been an uncomfortable walk home." I laughed as Bonnie took the scrubs from me.

"Yeah, no big deal. I know what you mean. It's one thing to shift but no one wants to flaunt around like that. Well, almost no one," Bonnie said, her eyes going somewhere over my shoulder.

I glanced behind me wondering what grabbed her attention only to see my older sister prancing around one of the injured warriors. If Manny's attitude was anything to judge their pack's culture from, I would guess that the warrior wasn't going to be a fan of her boobs hanging out. No matter how hard she tried to shove them into his face.

"I'm going to slip on out of here. Get me if you need anything." Shaking my head at the spectacle that was Stacy, my extra special sister, I turned to walk back out the door.

"Oh, Izzy, Izzy," came the loud voice of my sister as I made it halfway down the aisle. "There you are. I was meaning to stop over today to see you!" she squealed, running over and throwing her arms around my neck to rock me left and right in an overdramatic hug. "Oh my gosh, Izzy! Can you believe what happened last night? The whole thing is just scary. The witches attacking like that. It could have been us! I mean, what would we even do if the witches came here next? The thing is just so frightening, and you living so far away from us. You would be the first one to be attacked," Stacy babbled out in a rush.

"I don't know, Stacy." I just laughed in the awkwardness while she inched down the aisle.

"It's something that you should really think about. You know, it might be a good time to start looking to settle down. We're not getting any younger, and what would you do if the fighting comes here?"

"I don't know. Think of my virtue to keep me warm at night." I laughed at her turning quick to bolt out as she stood there reminding me of a gaping salmon.

I wondered if the boys would like salmon for dinner tonight. If I remember right, the fisherman brought in a ton of salmon yesterday from there catching. The fish were starting their swim downriver for the mating season.

The thought of the hungry mouths I'd have to feed later had me making my way to the store next. Thankfully that was a simpler trip than the rest of the morning. I got four full bags of groceries and started my way back to the cabin, ready to just sit and rest my eyes for a few minutes.

This dream, though, died right when I entered the tree lines only to have a shadow come out from behind; one of them with none other than Wayne. What did I do wrong to end up on his radar? Like really, he never spared me a glance before and now two times in one day. I must have angered the great moon goddess somehow. Or was it the witches? Did they curse me when I went up the mountain? A curse of insufferable conversation. Was that a thing?

"Wayne, what a surprise," I said, walking around him with my bags.

"Yes. I was hoping to run into you again," he said, falling into step next to me.

Look at him! What a gentleman! Walking with his hands in his pockets while I lugged four bags of groceries through the woods.

"Well, what do you want, Wayne?"

"I was hoping to talk to you about something actually."

Approaching my back door, I juggled the bags to get my keys. After all the company that morning, leaving the door unlocked just didn't seem wise to me, at least not until life calmed down and the pop and stops stopped.

"Wayne, I don't mean to be rude..." *Yes, I did*, I thought to myself. "But I have a lot of things that I have to get done today. Can you just ask me whatever it is that you want to ask?" *And go away*, I added in my head. At least I hoped it was just in my head, though at this point who knew.

"Look at you being all eager. I was hoping you would go to the moon's harvest bonfire with me?"

Shock hit me hard, and the words came out of my mouth with no thought, "No, I'm sorry but no." Slipping through the door and shutting it in his face.

What the hell is going on with people lately? They have lost their minds. Walking into other people's homes and running around like loons. It has to be the witches' magic because there was no other reason that made any sense for why everyone was losing it.

At least the rest of the day was quiet, and the boys came in just before nightfall. They ate dinner and got ready to sleep. I set up the living room for the boys and went to crash into my bed, hoping

26

tomorrow was nothing like today and that the world had gone back to sanity.

I was sliding into bed, ready to close my eyes for the night, only to have them open right away as the bedroom door opened and in walked the boys to stand at the side of the bed. I stared at them as they stared back. Tommy was the first to climb in next to me followed by quiet Danny, who I was coming to realize only spoke when he truly had something to say. Manny was the last one, who was more reluctant than the other two. Once they were all settled in for the night, I took a deep breath, closing my eyes again. Only to have Tommy tap me on the shoulder. Opening my eyes again, I looked over at him.

"Can you tell us a story?" Tommy asked with his big green eyes looking up at me.

"I'm sorry, sweetie, I don't think I know any. What kind of story do you want to hear?"

"Any kind is fine."

"Umm, well, let's see... Umm, once upon a time in a land far away stood a castle that housed the prettiest princess."

"Not a fairy tale," whined Manny from the far end of the bed. "I'm ten and fairy tales aren't real."

"Oh, yeah, how do you know they're not real? The stories had to come from somewhere, didn't they?" I said right back.

"Because if every she-wolf stood around waiting for a male to do something, they would never get the windows fixed, my auntie always said."

At that, I busted out into laughter not expecting that. Though I had to admit that he was right.

"Okay, hotshot, why don't you tell the bedtime story."

"Okay," Manny said and laid there for a few minutes, thinking only to sit up straight when it came to him. "Once long ago, up in the mountains lived the most feared monsters known as the Lucan."

"No scary stories. You boys do need to get some sleep at some point, and I think there have been enough scary things for you boys lately."

"It's not a scary story, I promise."

"Well, okay then. Let's hear it."

"Okay, where was I? Oh, right, lived the Lucan. They were feared warriors who possessed the power to not only shift into wolves but could shift into a beast form while keeping their human forms, standing on two legs. They had great power of both the supernatural and the magical.

"Once there was a great battle. A Lucan fell in love with a human woman. His brother, the leader of their clan, couldn't accept her among them, saying it would make half-breeds and weaken the bloodline. So the brother left with his half of the pack that over time broke off into smaller packs and continued to mix the bloodlines that caused the wolves of the moon goddess. It's believed that it was the wishes of the goddess to mix and spread throughout the world and grow. The history of the world's being written down with the prophecies that are meant to be fulfilled for the moon goddess were kept locked away by the last standing pure blood Lucan, the brother.

"The story goes of a great love. She had long brown hair down to her waist..." Manny started to yawn, and his words trailed off as he talked and drifted off to sleep.

I sat up slowly and looked at the other boys who had also fallen asleep before he probably even began. Though I had to admit, it was funny that his bedtime story was more like a history lesson. The boy needed some fun in his life. It couldn't be good to be so serious all the time.

I closed my eyes to drift off to sleep only to have my dreams take her somewhere else. Somewhere dark with wet air. I was walking moving through trees, winding around them like a snake in the night. There in the distance was a light. Small and blue. I moved closer, but with every step I took, it was like the light moved away.

Why must the light play with me? I just wanted to know what it was.

So I picked up my pace, moving faster and faster until I was running after the light, not watching where I was going, just staring straight at the light and feeling the air move across my face until I came to a river. The light dancing over the water was just out of reach, bobbing up and down like a fishing hook on a rough current.

The light started to move away, going over to the rock face. I followed, moving into the river, though I didn't feel the coldness of the water. I was so fixated on the shiny beacon in front of me.

Once I reached the rock face, I walked alongside it, keeping my hands on the stone wall to hold my balance. Why was I feeling so dizzy? I didn't know, but I was starting to wobble on my feet. All I knew was that I had to know where this light was going. The more I walked, the brighter the light got. I had to know what the light wanted to show me. The light looked like it had a pulse running through it. As I stared at the light, I became distracted, and my foot slipped off the cliff, and I started to slide down the cliff ledge. Falling over the edge of the cliff, there I dangled from my hands, clinging to the edge with my claws that came out to catch my fall. I tried to scream but no sound came from my mouth; I just dangled there with my mute mouth gapping open.

In the corner of my eye, there was the blasted light, dancing almost gleefully in the air. Not having to hang on, just floating freely without a care. The light started to move away from me again. Anger coursed through me.

How dare that light mock me? That's what it was doing, dancing there in the moonlight free as a bird. Somehow, I moved, putting one hand over the other, following the bloody blue light. Without a thought or a care, I was crab walking the cliff's edge. Determined and mad I was going to catch that ball if it was the last thing I ever did. Then I saw it…an opening in the cliff's wall. A cave with a light of a flame lighting up the entrance way. I walked my way over using all the muscles in my arms that were screaming in protest to the strain on them. My feet every once and while caught a small ledge in the wall to hold my weight for a few minutes.

Coming to the cave opening, the blue light moved inside, and I leaped from the cliff to land on the platform. Standing, I took a step into the cave. Looking around, all I could see were books and scrolls tucked away into the walls. Movement drew my attention away though. That little blue light was starting to shake. Almost shimmering in color now. Then the light at a speed that shocked me sprang forward right toward me. I stepped back not realizing I hadn't moved as far into the cave as I thought because the next thing I knew, I was falling through the air. I opened my mouth to scream, and this time I made noise. As loud as possible, a scream escaped me.

Then I felt it, hands grabbing at my arms, shaking me. I bolted up right in bed. I had sweat running down my back. I grabbed at the hands holding my arms as my surroundings came back to me. There, shaking me awake was none other than the Alpha Damien. The sun was high in the sky of a new day, and the clock read 9:00 a.m.

"How are you in my cabin!" Yelling at him was my first reaction as I started slapping at him, throwing a fit and not caring that we were now both sitting in my bed.

With my hair a mess and covered in sweat, no coffee, and company was not going to happen.

CHAPTER 4

GETTING OUT OF BED and ignoring the smirk that was on his face from my hollowing, I made my way to the kitchen, grabbing the coffeepot, and started to make the liquid of the heavens as aggressively as I could. I didn't even realize that everyone in the cabin made their way into the kitchen with me. I was too busy continuing my little snit. Thankfully, the coffeepot was an instant brew. I poured a cup for myself and one for Damien, hoping this will make up for yelling at him. I took a sip and sat down across from him, completely aware that yet again I was in my pajamas, but at this point, I couldn't seem to care. The dream was still playing in my mind. Going over the cliff had felt so real; I could have sworn I was actually falling.

We sat in silence for a few moments until he finally spoke. "I heard about your runs up the mountain, and I wanted to thank you for bringing the men down to get help."

"It's fine, no big deal really. I just kind of reacted."

"I have to ask how old are you? You don't look that old."

"I'm twenty actually so, no, not that old, but I'm a good runner."

"Tell me, how does a twenty-year-old get a cabin on her own down here without a mate? Or is there a man that I haven't heard about yet from the boys? I mean no disrespect."

The bluntness that he asked threw me for a surprise, and I started to laugh. Thinking about how I came into possession of the cabin though made me kind of sad for something lost.

"Well, I can tell you, but it's a bit of a story. And no, I have the cabin on my own. It's my cabin and trust me when I tell you the cabin likes it that way. The cabin used to belong to the seer of the pack before she passed. I used to come visit her when I was young. As I got older, so did she. I would stop by every day after school to help her around the cabin and in the woods. She would tell the most amazing stories. When she passed on, she had left me the cabin, telling my father, the alpha, that since I tend to it already that me having it and all the belongings inside wouldn't be that much different. He didn't know I spent so much time with her, and considering he thought she was a crazy old bat, he didn't like hearing exactly how much time I spent with her, though he couldn't argue that the cabin was to go to me. She wouldn't let him, insisting that the cabin wouldn't be housed by anyone but me," I told him.

And it was the truth, the cabin would not house anyone but me. The magical barriers around the land it was built on wouldn't keep people for long unless it liked them. Getting rid of them one way or another, however the land and trees saw fit.

The truth about the woman, though, was that she actually was crazy, and the cabin was proof of that. Well, it was on the edge of the pack lands; it is probably the safest of all the places to be. The woman was paranoid and made a point of setting up traps and tricks to any unwelcomed company that meant to do harm to those that took care of it. She would say in a wise voice that held more wisdom than sense, "You be good to the cabin, dearly, and the cabin will be good to you." She meant it.

Thinking back on the woman, I couldn't help but remember one time years ago, one of the men who hunt for the packs kept coming around and bothering the old woman. Until one day, the tree that stood just in front of her porch horsewhipped the man right on the ass. I was sitting on the porch with one of the woman's spell books, and I laughed so hard at the way he jumped and ran off. I fell off the rocker. She came out and told me to run the book inside before the alpha saw. It was forbidden to use magic in the pack lands. The punishment was banishment without hesitation. The elders of all the packs thought that it would just bring trouble from the forces of nature. Sure enough, the alpha came, and there we sat sipping on tea, talking about my lessons I had that day in class. That day, the woman swore me to secrecy about the books she kept hidden in the house. I never told anyone. Upon her passing, the cabin and all the things inside were left to me.

I still get sad when I think of her for the memories and lessons she left with me are worth more than anything. For thoughts of her are never far from my mind. It was a safe place, somewhere you go to hide like a sanctuary.

Realizing that I had drifted off into thought for who knew how long, I took a sip of my coffee.

"How old are you, if I may ask?"

"Twenty-five."

"Young for an alpha," while stating the fact, I stared right at him.

Something about him made it hard for me not to look him in the eye. Those eyes were unnerving but almost hypnotic. They were almost drawing me in. I got a sudden need to get closer to him, though I ignored it and just took another sip of my coffee. I had never felt a pull to someone like this before. I could only really blame it on all the things that were going on. It was like my mind was being whipped around by a tornado lately. I used to have very clear thoughts. I knew exactly what was going to happen and when. Now it was like my mind was a swarm of bees. I had no control over anything. No idea what was going to happen or what I was feeling. Looking into his eyes was dangerous because something about them made me feel safe. Trusting that feeling right now without really analyzing it didn't seem wise.

"I run the lands at the very top of the mountain. It's not much land but enough for us. We aren't as possessive of the running lands as you people seem to be."

"Us people?" I was kind of shocked at the way he said this, like we were so different from them.

Damien didn't say anything more though and just sat there and sipped his coffee. Apparently, it was his turn to be lost in thought. That was okay because little Tommy hopped right in to speak for his alpha. It seemed like something the boys did often. They looked used to doing the talking for Damien.

"Alpha Damien and the guys don't like to come to the flatlands. If they could have it their way, they wouldn't leave the woods at all."

"Is that so?" I asked, smiling at him. It was hard not to smile at the boy.

"We come down to fight, handle peace talks and seminars, then go back up to report everything that happens down here, so the old man can stay in the loop. I'm still a member of my father's pack. Though you know him as Alpha William," Damien added. "And yes, we would rather stay up in the mountains than come down. Though we come down when we're needed for a good fight."

"That's your father?" I thought, *Doesn't he only have one son though?* Trying to think back on what my father had said when he came home from the last Gathering of Alphas.

I never understood why they all gathered to talk about what the other packs had going on. From what Father always said, it was a waste of time. The alphas don't know what the other packs needed, but they had enough two cents to tell you what they thought you needed. If you were to ask me, I would think it would be a bad idea to have all that testosterone in one place. From the stories, more than one brawl had broken out at the meetings.

"Yeah, he actually has two. My brother is going to take over his lands. I'm not much for the being alpha part. Too much of a headache with all the drama they have to deal with."

"Damien's the head warrior. He's the alpha of the battle men," Manny said with such pride.

"I train the warriors and run the battles you mean," he said to Manny who also decided to jump in.

Though to be honest, I was just getting confused. If he was just a warrior and not an alpha, why was he called an alpha then and had his own land? Though he did give off the aura of an alpha without question. His presence alone demanded respect, holding a certain level of authority that couldn't be denied.

"If you're a warrior, where were you the night the witches came?"

"Away at conference along with my Bata, Keith. My third in command, Doc, was at some kind of seminar. There was no warning that something was coming. The witches never made contact. They just attacked. I can't think of a reason why they would suddenly want to fight us," Damien said.

I realized that when he was thinking hard on something, the scar running down his chin seemed to stand out more as his jaw clenched.

"You were all gone when the witches came. The twins left too after you three left," said Tommy, and Damien's eyes had a flash behind them at this news.

I wanted to know who the twins were, but the look that came over Damien's face made me not want to ask.

"That's probably why the witches came when they did. The Rapture wasn't there to hold the mountain." This came from Manny who held his head higher with the pride for his leader. Though he was only ten, there was a wiseness to him that came from years of listening in.

But it got me thinking...

If they were all away from the post, that must mean the witches were watching the lands somehow or that someone on the inside was talking to them. Considering they didn't like leaving their homes, I would think that would mean they don't venture down often. Even Manny said, "the Doc" only comes down every two months for supplies. The timing would have been planned, or the witches just got lucky otherwise. If all the main warriors stood with Damien, being away would explain why the main pack fell within a night. Damien and his men must have the control of all the lands just by the muscle they possess. Though this didn't make much sense to me because it was different down here. There was no way I was going to ask him to explain why the most feared land in the territory could fall so easily because they were gone. You would think that Alpha William's pack would have some fighters in it too. From what I saw that night, though, they had fought the best they could. It was hard to really remember that you couldn't see where the attacks were coming from. Everything was happening so fast; it was a blur. I just didn't understand why all this distraction had to happen. None of it really made sense, and the harder I tried to think about it, the more I needed aspirin.

"How many people are in your pack?" There, that was a safer question.

"Twelve guys total are with me, and I should be going. Some of them will be showing up soon to figure out what the next steps should be." He made it all the way to the door only to stop and turn around to look straight at me. "Unless of course I can hold my war meeting here?"

Though his face was completely straight, I thought for sure he had to be joking with me, but at this point in life, who knew?

"No, oh, no, no, no. There will be no war meetings in my living room." I suddenly really wanted him to leave before others came looking for him. I was starting to learn when you let these people in, they keep coming back.

"What about the kitchen?"

"Out. Now out! No meetings in the living room, the kitchen, the bedroom, not even on the roof. Out." As I ranted, I walked toward him, opening the door, and started to shove him back.

He backed out, though I wasn't silly enough to think I was making him. If he didn't want to move, I was sure he wouldn't have been.

"Really? Not even the bedroom?"

And with that, I shut the door in his face with enough force to shake my flowers on the counter. I could have sworn the flowers were laughing at me in this moment of time. I must have looked a sight. I didn't even bother to answer that question in my sudden haste to close the door on him. He just unnerved me to the point where I couldn't even tell if he was joking or not. My mind was running wild. I stood there for a few minutes trying to put my thoughts in a proper order.

Yes, the witches cursed me up on that mountain that night. It was the only explanation for the twilight zone my life has become. Somewhere, my quiet unnoticeable life had gotten all turned around. Who would have thought that dealing with three children would be easier than some grown men?

The rest of the day passed by in a flash with no real excitement. This was something I was really happy for. The boys and I were just reading in the living room and settling down from the day's activities.

I had the boys outside with me to water the trees and do yard work. I showed them how to spread around the coffee grounds and use tea leaves as fertilizer for the flowers. Danny really took a lot of interest in yard care. He helped trim back the bushes so the leaves would stay healthy. I taught them about the different flowers. I had planted a batch of herbal flowers that would help with healing. Bonnie wanted to start mixing her own remedies. She was given a medicine book from one of the witch doctors she trained with for a month last summer. I told the boys some of the stories I remembered her telling me. The boys seemed fascinated with hearing about what the plants could do. So we spent most of the day outside going over every plant.

Once back inside and settling down from a day of fresh air, I had to explain again that I didn't have a TV because I just didn't want a TV. Children…they seemed to really miss the television from home. It took some talking into, but I managed to convince them that reading a book was the same thing as watching TV. The only difference was that the movie played in your head and not off some screen. Then they finally settled in and got comfortable with their own books. I was really happy that Zella had saved some of my easier books from when I was younger.

When there was a knock on the front door, it made the room groan as a whole. Guessing it was safe to say the boys weren't liking all the company here as much as me. Manny was the one to get up and get the door.

"Well, hey there little man, is the lady of the house here?" I heard Wayne's voice and growled to myself. He sounded like a patronizing twat when he spoke to the boy.

I knew it wasn't going to win any favors though. I also knew that Manny had a surprisingly short fuse. The night had been so peaceful.

I was just starting to get up when I heard Manny's answer, "No." Just that one word and then the front door slammed shut.

I spun around to see Manny coming back into the room with his hands full of flowers and a blank expression on his face.

"Manny, who was at the door?" I asked not quite sure how to handle this boy. I didn't know whether to laugh or scold him.

"Some guy," he said with a shrug. It was like he didn't have a care in the world.

"Umm, what did he want?" I was trying to think of the best way to approach him in conversation, but I found it hard to talk to Manny. I really didn't know how he would react to certain moments.

"I don't know." Setting the flowers down on the table and shrugging again. The blank look on his face was never changing.

How a little one could be so compact in his reactions was truly just unnerving.

"Manny, you do know you can't slam the door in people's faces, right?" I decided to go with the gentle approach.

"Why not?"

"Because it's rude. Don't they teach you manners up in those mountains of yours?"

"But I don't really like him." Now he just looked confused as if what I was saying didn't make any sense to him.

"That is not the point. The point is that you can't just snatch flowers out of someone's hand and slam the door in their face."

"But I did."

"Exactly and you can't do that."

"But I did do it. So I can do it technically, right?"

Exasperated with the way the conversation was going, I just threw my hands up and figured I would have to talk to Damien about the etiquette lessons I had just decided to sign Manny up for in the morning.

"Well, you shouldn't do it. Anyway, it's late. You boys should head off to bed. Go on," I said, shooing the boys out of the living room.

I sat back down on the couch and picked up the cup of tea.

I was sitting alone now and having the dream from the night before come back again to the front of my mind. Something about it left a feeling that told me I didn't really want to go back to sleep. Something was just off about it. Though I couldn't quite put my figure on what was wrong. As I sat there playing it over again in my head for what had to be the hundredth time of the day, I saw something out of the corner of my eye. Jumping nearly out of my skin, I swung my head around to the blue orb bouncing around in the air, swinging toward the bookshelf. Now I knew I wasn't dreaming. I slowly got to my feet to move closer to the thing. Yeah, because doing that in my sleep was such a great idea. Why not give it a go while being awake?

This time, though, the orb didn't run away. It settled on a book that was sitting on the shelf, and when I noticed the book, I could have fainted right then and there. All the blood ran from my body as adrenaline started to kick in. It was a different kind of adrenaline from the other night. I didn't feel the need to fight or flight, but the shock in the book the orb picked to land on brought back memories. *Pride and Prejudice* was the one book that opened the trap in the wall. It would take you into Zella's secret room where she kept all her special books and things she collected. Taking a deep breath and looking behind me to make sure the boys hadn't gotten up, I pulled the book down, opening the door to the room I couldn't bring myself into since I moved into the cabin. The room smelled just like her perfume—patchouli.

CHAPTER 5

"WELL, IT'S ABOUT TIME you came a visited me, girly," the voice came from the air.

I completely froze where I was standing. It didn't come from the air; it came from the orb. The orb, the same one that was in my dream, was now in the hidden room, and it was speaking.

With this, I just turned and walked out of the room staring straight ahead until I made my way into the kitchen. Grabbing the tea kettle, I filled it with some water and got the calming herb tea ready. Once the fresh cup was ready, I took it back into the living room to sit on the couch and stared at the now open doorway. I couldn't see the orb or smell the perfume anymore.

I knew that voice and I knew what was in that room. The crazy old bat passed away and left it all to me. Ms. Zella couldn't be speaking to me though. I had wished so many times after she passed that I could talk to her one last time. Now hearing her voice again, it was just too much to think about. So here I sat staring at the doorway only to see the blue orb come back out of the room and move to float next to me. The orb didn't speak this time; it just floated there as if waiting for me to make a move.

There is nothing in this house that will hurt you, dear. Though I can't say the same for others. Don't be afraid, I thought in my head, though I knew that wasn't my own voice rattling away up there.

Somehow though, hearing random voices in my head seemed less scary than hearing them out loud. At that thought, I couldn't hold in a giggle. Maybe I can be the next crazy old bat and completely follow Zella's footsteps. I was already halfway there clearly.

Downing a big gulp of tea, I stood up, putting my shoulders back, and walked into the room.

It was left exactly the same, though it did need a dusting. The blue orb floating in and moved in front of me, going over to a part of the shelves that held the history books. I went and grabbed the one it was floating by. I looked over the cover. It was a hard leather book that didn't have a title on it. Tucking it under my arm, I looked around the room before my eyes began to cloud with tears.

"I miss you, Ms. Zella," I said before I turned with my book and fled the room. Sadness at the memories were coming back in a rush.

I sat on the couch and opened the book to begin reading and reading. The story was set in a time many years ago, and the wording was in old English, and there were spells written into the pages. I recognized them as spells because they were worded just the way Zella's special books were. Versus some that weren't in English but an old dead language that Zella had taught me when I'd spend time with her. At least I always thought it was a dead language, but flipping through the pages, I really had to wonder. One story caught my attention, and I stopped skimming.

It was about two brothers who saw the future of the world differently. There was a massive battle between the two, and it divided a nation. There were sides going in opposite ways never to speak again. The story said when the brothers got older, they wanted to mend the drift between them, but neither one of them took steps to heal the damage that was caused. I couldn't help but scoff at the idea that two men were too pigheaded to admit they were wrong.

Lost in the story, I didn't see the lightning that was dancing in the trees. It wasn't until little Tommy came running into the living room with Manny and Danny right behind him. The boys ran to the couch where I was curled up. I closed the book and stuffed it behind the pillow I was laying back on. They were all talking at once, and it was hard to follow what they were trying to tell me.

"What's wrong?" I asked the boys.

The fear that was in Tommy's eyes wasn't something I had seen since the night I grabbed him from the woods. But before they could answer, the back door swung open so hard it smashed into the wall, making a hole in the drywall.

"Let's go now!" Damien barreled his way in barking orders.

I turned to tell him where he could shove his orders, but the words died in the back of my throat at what I saw behind him. Lightning with sparks of blues and purples were flying through the trees as large wolves were charging into the woods, moving toward the sparks. The crackling and popping were so loud there was no mistaking it for a tree trunk cracking. The witches were here.

Damien turned around, barking orders at wolves I didn't recognize. I just simply reacted, scooping little Tommy up, and I ran for the bookshelves. I could hear Zella in my head telling me to get to the bookshelf. This was my home, and how dare they think to come here!

Nothing can touch you here, girly, Zella's voice rang out strong in my head.

I knew I was moving and doing things, but I wasn't thinking. I was just reacting. It felt like I was on autopilot.

"Let's go, move!" I yelled at the other two boys who moved to stand right next to me.

They looked terrified as the noises of battle grew louder until it sounded like it could have been right outside my back door. A glance out the window showed the flashes were still a bit away. I pulled the book to the safe room and ran inside with the boys right on my heels.

"Stay here, don't move, and stay quiet. Okay?" I told the boys, setting Tommy down.

Manny moved to put his arms around Tommy as the boy started crying. Watching the three of them move to huddle together, something sparked inside of me, and I felt angry. Angry at the fact that they brought this to the cabin. The cracking of the trees added gas to the anger that was bubbling until it was a blinding rage.

"Zella," I said out loud. "Zella!" I said again.

If I saw her once, hopefully she'll come back now.

"Zella!" At this point, it was almost a scream.

"Child, I'm right here." The blue orb formed in the corner.

The boys almost fell over at the sight of it. Their eyes grew large. Manny moved to stand in front of Danny, and Tommy, I put my hand on his shoulder to calm him.

"You've always been good to the land. Let the land help you. Go. You remember, don't you?"

I stood there for a few minutes trying to think, but my brain didn't want to do more than scream in rage. Until the crack of another tree had me turning, my wolf was madder than ever before. I turned in a blackened rage and made my way to the porch.

"Damien."

"Why are you still here! Get the boys and leave."

"I'm not leaving my lands." The voice that came from me wasn't mine anymore. It was calm and lower. "Pull the wolves out of my trees."

"Isabel, are you insane? Leave."

"No. Pull the wolves back. I'm not leaving."

"What the hell are you doing?"

I was making my way to the trees just outside of the porch. He tried to grab my arm, but I ripped it away. I did remember. Walking up to the biggest of the trees, I put my hand on the trunk, saying the prayer of the lands that Zella used to say every time we fed the grounds. The same prayer I said when I fertilized the grounds earlier today with the boys. Stepping back, I opened the book I grabbed before running out the room. I didn't even remember grabbing it, and if I was being honest with myself, I didn't even know the page I was turning to. It was like something else was moving my hands, turning the pages. Once I was on the page I wanted, I started reading out loud.

As I read, the tree started to move, swaying back and forth until the branches started swinging and creaking. Damien was yelling something, but I didn't pay him any mind. Suddenly, the wolves were charging back out of the woods, fleeing the tree lines. Once the last wolf was free and clear, the tree lit up. The trunks were growing and moving. The flashes were getting brighter, but when the trees screamed their rage, the flashes stopped. I moved to the center of the porch and turned to a different page. Again, my hands acting all on their own. I started reading. I didn't know the words that were coming out of my mouth; it was almost like I was possessed.

I knew it was Zella guiding me, and it gave me great comfort knowing this. Once I finished speaking, the winds picked up and blew so hard I almost fell down the steps. Strong arms wrapped around my waist was the only thing that kept me from meeting the ground. Between the winds and the swinging trees, the forest put on a magnificent show that went on for what felt like forever. The whole time, Damien never let go of my waist. I just read incantations and incantations, sending them straight at the attackers.

When the trees and wind finally stopped, no one came out of the woods. The silence that came over the atmosphere seemed deafening. We just stood there, neither one of us speaking. The witches never came out of the tree lines. I didn't know what to say and how to explain what he just saw. Once the silence came, the threat at that moment was gone. The anger drifted away, and I didn't feel relief; I felt dread. I had just broken a very big law of our people. So instead of speaking, I moved away from him and walked back over to the tree. The same tree I climbed as a child, the tree that housed me after my first broken heart, felt my tears when I buried the cat I had taken as a pet when I was younger. I walked to the tree, touching it and thanking it for standing tall. Then I took a deep breath, turned, and walked back into the cabin with Damien following behind me.

Still not speaking, I went to check on the boys. They were still in the room.

"Hey, guys, it's safe to come out now," I said, moving so they could come out.

Much to my surprise, when they came out, they didn't say anything; they just started to make their way back to the bedroom.

"You guys okay? Do you want to talk about what just happened?"

They stopped walking and looked at me. They didn't look scared or upset, just tired. Tommy broke away and came over, wrapping his arms around my waist.

"We're fine, just tired. Thank you for scaring them away," Tommy said, looking up at me with a small smile and turned walking out of the room with the other two boys.

"Don't worry about them. I had a talk with them when you were rattling the brains out of those women." Laughed the orb of Zella.

"What the hell!" Damien jumped, eyes shifting and claws coming out.

His reaction made me react, still on high alert from what had just happened. I snarled right back and moved in front of Zella. Though instead of putting me in my place for snarling at him which would have been a normal reaction of an alpha, he settled back on his heels and rubbed his neck.

Taking a deep breath, I figure it was best to just get this whole mess out of the way. "I guess we have some things to talk about. I'm not sure where to start though."

CHAPTER 6

"WELL, LET'S START BY sitting down. How does that sound?" Damien said, which was probably a good sign. I hope.

Though I didn't know him well enough to know if it was the clam before the storm or if he was going to be open-minded.

"Why don't I put on some tea."

"Okay, tea sounds good." He gestured with his hands to lead the way, so I moved down the hallway toward the kitchen.

Putting the pot on, I turned around to find him sitting at the kitchen table watching me.

"Umm, I honestly don't know what to say." And I truly didn't. For once in my life, I was at a complete loss for words.

"Okay. Why don't you start at the beginning?" Damien said, trying to be helpful, but I laughed silently.

"I don't even know where the beginning is. Look, I don't practice magic and I don't know spells."

"Were we standing on the same porch? You can't backtrack that, Isabel."

"No. What I mean is that the book wasn't even mine. What I'm trying to say is, well, I don't know."

"Oh, shush, child." The blue orb came into the kitchen floating over the table. "The books were mine, boy."

"Zella, I can handle this," I said with a small smile coming to my face.

Having her here even in this form was more than I ever could have asked for.

"Zella as in the crazy she-wolf that used to own the cabin?"

"Who are you calling crazy? I was sane enough to raise an amazing girl here, wasn't I?"

"I just meant—"

"Now who's backtracking," Zella cut him off, and the blue orb started to shimmer in what I would have sworn was happiness.

"You're loving every minute of this, aren't you?" I asked the orb unable to help myself.

"Yes, I've rested for too long. A little excitement is good."

"Yes, but I think this might be a conversation that I need to have with him."

"Yeah, yeah, but you didn't know how to start it so let me help." With that, the blue orb swung right in Damien's face and let loose. "The books and cabin were mine. Isabel was left with them when I passed, and if you're going to be the big bad alpha and punish someone for the belongings or the things you saw here tonight, you can punish me," the blue orb challenged seeming to grow in size almost.

Damien just put his hands up in surrender.

"Zella, please."

"All right I said my piece. I'll go check on the boys." With that, the orb moved out of the room, vanishing down the halls.

Damien looked slightly alarmed at her parting words.

"The boys will be fine. She's harmless."

"That wasn't harmless, what I saw."

"Well, she won't harm the boys. I swear."

"Let's just start with the beginning."

Setting down the two cups of tea, I took a seat across from him. "Ask away and I'll do my best to answer. At this point, what do I have to hide? I have one condition, though, before we start this conversation."

"What would that be?"

"Anything that I answer right now will be honest. All I want is your promise that it will stay between us. Please don't tell my father. He disliked Zella greatly, and I don't want her memory harmed. She was an amazing woman that meant the world to me. And I don't want people knowing about me or the books. It's a promise I made when I was young for this secret to be kept. A promise I fully intend to keep."

"All right, that sounds fair enough." To his credit, he did pause to think before asking the first question. "Umm, let's start off easy. When did you learn you could do magic?"

"That is not easy." I laughed "I don't really know Zella taught me a little here and there when I was growing up."

"Like the stuff that happened on the porch?"

"No, not like that. Stuff like waking up the trees and moving water around. Small stuff like that."

"Waking up a tree is small?"

"Well, yeah. I can't do things like those witches can. Just simple defense stuff. Zella knew a lot more than me. She would always say that you had to take care of yourself because you didn't always know when help would come."

"Magic is forbidden among our people."

"Yes. Though we all have it in us. Magic is what gives us our wolves. Once upon a time, magic was in our everyday lives. It was even written about in our history books."

"That's impossible. There are no history books written about our kind. That's why we have pack storytellers. It would be too dangerous to let the books fall in the wrong person's hands."

"Well, you see that isn't actually true. There are books. Hold on a moment." I got up from the table and went into the living room, grabbing the book I was reading before everything went insane. Bringing it back into the kitchen, I didn't hand it to him. I just held it to my chest when I took my seat again. "You see, there are books of our kind's beginning history. When we were one pack, one nation. The pups' tales that have been told from generation to generation are actually true. Just changed over time as the story was retold." I set the book on the table with my hand on the leather cover.

He reached across the table to take it, and I tightened my hand on it for a moment.

"Gentle. It's old and belonged to Zella. It was in her room."

"The hidden room you put the boys in?"

"Yes." Still not letting go of the book.

"I'll be careful. I promise." He tried to give me a smile, I think, to lighten the mood in the room, but it had little effect on me on letting the book go.

It wasn't until he put his hand on mine. The shock it gave me was what had me jerk my hand away. Damien took the opportunity and snatched the book up, ignoring the feeling that just happened, though I could have sworn I saw his wolf peek out in his eyes.

They used to say that when you found your true mate, you'd feel an electrical current. Though I always took that as a fairy tale they told little ones. To find a true mate was rare and to find one that didn't reject you or hurt you in some way was even rarer. Just look at Zella. She had found her true mate only to have him turn his back on her for someone else simply because he wanted power, to move up higher in the ranks. Something that he wouldn't have been able to do if he had kept his destined mate. She lived with the heart broken for the rest of her days. Knowing that her true mate thought she was lowly on the ranking pool, Zella left her pack, moving here to get away from him and the sad looks of her pack mates. Here she learned to stand alone and showed me that it was better to be alone. As I got older and watched my sister make a fool of herself all for a male's attention, I realized how true she was. The hunt for a mate made women lose themselves to appear more appealing.

So I did the most logical thing I could think of. I ignored it. I ignored what I thought that shock meant. It wasn't something that I was going to waste my time on anymore. Though as I told myself that, I couldn't help but wonder if he felt it too or had the same thoughts about what it was that I did.

"This is amazing," he said, pulling me from my thoughts.

"In the book, there is a mention of a library. It's tucked away in the mountain side. I think I need to go there."

"Why would you think that?"

"Do you remember when you broke into my cabin, and I was screaming in my sleep? I had a dream, but I don't think it was a dream because Zella was in it. As the orb, not as, well, Zella. Anyway, I think it was a premonition, not a dream."

"Do you get premonitions?"

"Sometimes. Though it's more like déjà vu. This was the first time it really felt like something different than that. I know it wasn't a dream. It didn't feel like a dream at all, and before that, I had never seen an orb. Something is telling me that I have to go to the cave. I need to find it."

"Why were you screaming? If it was a premonition, what made you scream?"

"I fell."

"You what?"

"I fell, over the cliff at the entranceway of the cave."

"And you want to go there? Have you lost your mind?" Now he yelled. Up until now, he hadn't lost his temper.

"Shh, you'll wake the boys."

At this point, we were both standing, coming to our feet almost simultaneously.

"Look, I know how this sounds but I have to go there. I know I do. I'm not sure why, and I can't really explain it. But I need to try and find the cave. There is a reason why I had that dream, and there is no way to know what it was actually about unless I go."

"Well then, I'll come with you."

"No, you weren't there in the dream."

"Oh, the dream where you fell off a cliff? That dream?"

"There is no need to be an ass and, yes, that dream. I have to go alone."

"What about the boys? They won't let the other women take care of them. They rather settle on you."

"What about their mothers? Surely, they have family besides me? I'm happy to have them here, but someone has to be looking for them."

At this, Damien went quiet for a few minutes, thinking of what to say.

Though what he came up with wasn't what I was expecting. "They don't really have any family. They stay in the pack house by me."

"How do they not have family?"

"They came from other packs all around the flatlands."

"I think it's your turn to start telling a story. How do you just acquire children?"

"My men and I come down to help other packs in times of war. They send messages up, stating their case for support if another pack is trying to take over for no reason other than personal gain. Like pack police. We don't answer to any packs other than our own. Just to keep it fair."

"Right, I know all this. You guys are like the boogeymen that will come get you if you step out of line or break laws. Which doesn't explain how you ended up being the guardian of children. Now that I'm thinking about it, it doesn't explain what gives you the right to watch over other packs keeping them in line," I said the last with air quotes because it just seemed fitting.

"I'm going to put this bluntly. We watch over and step in because we don't actually care what happens to the flatlands. We just protect the privacy of our people and ways. We are direct descendants of the original Lucan. They came with us willingly. The parents had fallen in different battles. I don't take all the children, just the ones that need somewhere to go. A lot of people take the lost children in. I just take the ones that won't get taken in."

"You're telling me no one wanted them?" I found this completely heartbreaking. "How can no one want them?"

"Manny bit everyone, unable to be controlled after the loss of his mother, and Danny followed his brother wherever he went. You couldn't separate them. Tommy was thought to be too small to make a strong wolf. Well, he could make a good omega when he grows up, plus he grew on me. Watching him age though, I don't think he's going to be an omega when he grows up. I know that for sure. There is something very different about him from other pups. I can't really put my finger on what it is though."

"How do you know he wouldn't be an omega, and I don't think he's different. He's just a sweet little boy."

"One he wouldn't leave his brother. Omegas even as pups don't fight back, and he wouldn't leave his brother. The fact they have been apart for this long just shows they want to stay here. I put money on when his brother is healed. You'll have another one to look after. Two trust me when he gets angry, there is something different about him. You don't see it often, but there is something growing in him. I don't know what, but I do know he's safer with us than with other packs that will use him for whatever gift he has."

"You don't shun gifts?"

"No." He laughed now, relaxing and putting his hands on my shoulders. "And I won't shun yours either. Yes, our people don't like magic, but the way I see it, you were taught out of the love of a woman, not for the harm of others. I think if you wanted to harm us or use it to hurt us, you would have when I came in uninvited. You wouldn't have told me to pull the wolves out of the woods if you didn't care for their safety. Taking the boys in and hiding them, defending them when the attack came to your own back door. You ran into a war just to save whoever you couldn't without any thought. I don't think there is any need to condemn you or tell others about your abilities. The secrets of you and Zella are safe."

"Oh." Lame but it was the only thing I could think to say.

Slowly, we made our way to the living room still talking about this and that. He told me about Tommy and what made him seem different from normal children. I heard stories I had to agree that he was definitely different, but I would want to see for myself before speculating. The stories of trying to find a home for Manny had me honestly laughing. I didn't need to hear them to know Manny was a handful but hearing them honestly made me want to keep him all the more. It sounded like he just needed love. Not smothering.

I told him stories about Zella and growing up with her. I told him about my sister and about Wayne's repeat visits. He laughed at hearing about Manny slamming the door in the guy's face. Though he stopped laughing when his eyes caught the flowers sitting on the table. Goddess, that felt like forever ago when it happened. I couldn't believe it was just earlier that night. We talked until we fell asleep, sitting on either side of the couch together.

CHAPTER 7

WHEN I WOKE UP, Damien wasn't on the couch anymore. Though I was lying fully on the couch, and I had a blanket covering me up. It was the one from my closet. I looked at it and smiled because Zella made it. I remembered when she made it. It was the only time she had ever crocheted, and some of the words she sprouted were some I had never heard before and hadn't heard since. I don't think they were English either. Though the blanket was a pretty green, the color of grass. She had put little balls throughout the pattern.

One time when I was sick and she was watching me, I slept on this couch, and she covered me up with the blanket. I laid there playing with the lumps, turning them inside out and back again. She made me my favorite dinner, au gratin with diced up ham steak. She always put a little extra butter than what the recipe called for.

Getting up, I folded the blanket with care and was in the process of laying it over the back of the couch then made my way to the kitchen where I found all three boys sitting at the table, and Damien was at the stove cooking.

One the boys looked at me, and they said together, "Good morning!"

I have to say they seemed more cheerful than I thought they would have. They didn't look scared or worried or at all traumatized.

"Good morning. How did you boys sleep?"

"We slept fine, Ms. Isabel," Manny said as he sat up straight in his chair like a perfect gentleman.

Tommy got up and went over to the counter. Standing on his tiptoes, he reached for the coffeepot.

"Honey, what are you doing? I can get that," I said making my way over to him.

"That's okay, I got it," he said, pouring a cup of coffee and turning around, handing it to me.

"Maybe you should have a seat and ask them how their bedtime stories were?" Damien said with more amusement in his voice, making me very curious.

"All right then…" Taking a seat and facing them head-on, I said, "Tell me about your bedtime stories."

"Ms. Zella told us the story of the dragon."

"A dragon?"

"Yeah, there was a princess that was held prisoner in a big tower, and the guards wouldn't let her out. And this great dragon shift flew up to her window. He charmed her with his sparkling scales until she climbed onto his back," Manny told me, and Tommy was quick to chime in.

"Then they lived happily ever after up in a volcano."

"Did you know a volcano is a large land mass that sticks out of the ground like a mountain, but a hot liquid comes out of it?" Danny added, shocking me because he didn't talk much.

"Yeah, and most mountains were once volcanos," Tommy said.

"Though some mountains come from the land plates sliding together over a lot of years." This came from Manny.

"Oh my, it sounds like it was a good story night," I said, looking over at Damien, but he was focusing on the stove cooking breakfast.

I couldn't quite see his face, though I got a good look of the scar that was down the side of his neck. To be honest, since the first time I met him, I never really noticed it anymore. Looking at him now without him knowing, I do have to admit it made him look charming. I looked away from him and took a sip of my coffee as the boys talked among themselves. They seemed happy and content. Considering all the events from last night, it was hard not to notice that something was just off at this moment.

Damien started serving plates of food when the back door opened and in waltzed Wayne, though he froze at the scene in front of him.

"Well, this is different. Isabel, you sure have been having a house full lately." He laughed and proceeded to walk into the kitchen and came around the table. He put his hands on the back of my chair.

I felt my back shift when he settled there. He wasn't always so creepy, but something changed in him lately, and well, I have a lot on my mind. I think I should have to address this because it was getting out of hand. Before the night the witches attacked the first time, he had never been here. I didn't understand why he started to come around now. Normally, he would only hang around my sister.

"Wayne, why don't we talk in the living room." I slid my chair back, slamming it into him, so he was forced to move away.

"That would be nice," he said following me into the living room.

Once there, I turned to face him ready to get this nonsense over with only to find Manny standing behind Wayne with his arms crossed and a scowl on his face.

"Manny, why don't you go back into the kitchen, honey?"

"Why?"

"Because Wayne and I are going to have a talk, and it would be very helpful if you went to the kitchen and watched the other boys. Besides, Damien could probably use some help navigating the kitchen," I said, shooing him back down the hallway.

"You sure have your hands full lately," Wayne said, laughing as Manny stomped back down the hallway, clearly unhappy that he was sent away.

I turned back to Wayne. For some reason, instinct told me not to keep my back to him. I never thought of him as anything more than a member of the pack that was just, you know, around some-times. He really was just someone that was around in passing, so to have to spend this much time dealing with him was not something I was used to, and I really didn't want to get used to it.

"What do you want, Wayne?"

"I just stopped to say hi and see if you needed anything. How long until the boys go back to where they belong? They have been staying with you for a while now."

"They are welcome to stay here for however long they want to, Wayne."

"Of course but you should start thinking about the future, especially with the witches running around on high dose of PMSs, and you know the mating moon is right around the corner."

"Mating moon! You have to be kidding me? Who is thinking of the mating moon right now? I have three boys to take care of, and the witches just attacked my back door just last night. I haven't even had a chance to look at the damages they did to my trees."

"I'm thinking of the mating moon, and I promise you so is that, well, that thug standing in your kitchen."

"He is not a thug. He's an alpha of the mountains that govern these lands and deserves your respect. Respect that you should give him before he gets cranky and knocks your teeth in if you want my advice."

"Now, Izzy, do you hear yourself? That isn't you talking, sweetie."

"Sweetie! Since when do you call me sweetie! When the witches attacked, did I hit my head or something?"

He laughed and grabbed my arms, rubbing them up and down. "You need to think about your future. You don't want to end up like the crazy old bat, do you? That's what that guy is going to leave you like.

"There was nothing wrong with Ms. Zella or the life that she had. She lived an exciting life with few regrets."

"Izzy, Izzy, let's not get sidetracked here. We're talking and you and me, the kind of pair we would make."

"Make as in together? Wayne, you and me have never even really talked before. You don't know anything about me as a person. What makes you think that we belong together?" I said, moving away from him to get him to stop rubbing me.

"Isabel, think about it. With you at my side, the alpha, your father, would consider me for the next in line to take over when he's ready to step down. He only had daughters, no sons to follow in his footsteps. Together we could run the pack and take over the surrounding lands. The power we could gather around us would be far more than what that back mountain thug could give you."

"That sounds absolutely ridiculous. One he is not a thug. He is an alpha and deserves the respect of one. Two you cannot run a land with an unwilling mate. It's a good way to find an early grave. Three the boys aren't going anywhere unless they wish, and four, which I think is the most important fact in the long list of reason why you ran idiot right now, is that I truly don't like you. I'm sorry if this sounds harsh, but I think full honesty right now is best. You spend more time chasing after my sister's than you ever did talking to me. And I think we should go back to that. I don't know what I did to suddenly get your attention, but I'm sorry, Wayne, I truly have no interest in being your mate. So if you have some grand ideal about the mating season, please do both of us a favor and just forget it." As I listed of all the reasons, my voice was growing louder. Before I knew what happened, I was yelling at him.

"Isabel, you need to think of your future. Those boys aren't going to be staying with you forever. Maybe it's a good idea to start separating yourself from them. They shouldn't be a part of your life's decisions, and you need to think of the years down the road. You're going to need a guy to take care of you. Why not pick the guy that has plans already in place to get what he wants?"

Before I could answer, there was an honest to goddess roar coming from the hallway. I spun around to see little Tommy, who had fangs and eyes shifted. Before I could react, he was charging across the living room and lunging for Wayne's head. He latched on, scratching with claws. He wasn't doing any real damage, but that didn't matter to Wayne. He ripped the boy off his head and threw him across the room. Tommy bounced off the wall and landed on the floor. When he landed, he crouched down ready to leap into the air again, but before he could, I had shifted, slammed into Wayne with the full weight of my wolf, taking him to the ground. Unlike the attack of Tommy though, I caused damage. Crouched on top of him, I bit and scratched until Wayne kicked me across the room, shifting into his own wolf, and he lunged for me.

Before he could make contact though, a large black wolf, larger the Wayne's wolf, was flying over the couch, grabbing him by the throat and slamming Wayne into the coffee table. The impact of the fall smashed the table into pieces. They fought rolling around on the floor toward the front door. Manny ran to the door and opened it wide just as the two rolled out the door and into the front yard. I shifted back to human and ran over to Tommy, who was sitting on the floor crying. As I crouched down next to him, Danny came around the corner with my robe and handed it to me.

"Tommy, are you okay?"

"Are you going to send us away?"

"Absolutely not! You guys are welcome to stay with me for as long as you want. Wayne is an idiot and he's wrong."

The boy was still crying and started to hug me tightly. "I like it here."

"Wayne is an ass," Manny said, coming to stand by us.

"Manny, mind your mouth, and yes, yes, he is. He has some grand thought that will never happen in a million years. I don't know where he got those thoughts from, but I would never choose him for a partner." I picked little Tommy up and moved to the couch. "Tommy, can I ask you something?"

"Yes, Ms. Isabel?" he said into my shoulder, the tears finally slowing down.

"Sweetie, do you know what you are? What your parents' animals were?"

"Yes," Tommy said in a small voice.

"Honey, what were their animals?"

"You'll get rid of me."

"No, I won't. I said you are welcome here for as long as you all wanted to stay, and I meant that. I don't say things that I don't mean, Tommy. Now what animals were your parents? It's important. I need to know, Tommy, or I wouldn't be asking. I'll watch after you regardless of the animals you have."

Tommy took a deep breath and rubbed his head on my shoulder. "Mom was a wolf," he said then tightened his arms even more around my neck. "Dad is a lion."

"A lion?" Shock came clear in my voice, causing Tommy to look up into my eyes.

"Mom met him when she went to school down south. She told me the story. They had a class together and fell in love. He didn't care she was a wolf and not a lioness, and Mom didn't care that he was a lion. They were happy. Mom's family didn't approve of him though because of it. Grandma got sick, and Mom came back up to help take care of her and say her goodbyes. She had brought me with to meet them. They didn't want me though because I'm a mixed breed. Then the packs attacked, and Mom died protecting me because they wouldn't let me into the safe house. When the fighting started, I sprouted my teeth. Alpha Damien took me in when the fighting stopped."

"Is your father alive then?"

"Yeah, but I don't remember where I'm from. I was four years old when it happened. I remember him and I know his name is Shawn. But I don't know where he lives."

I put my arms around him and held him to me. "Well, when this is all said and done, why don't we find him together and go from there? Look, you're stuck with me, kid, whether you want to be or not. All of you are stuck with me."

At that point, the front door opened, and a muddy Damien walked with new scratches and bruises. He had a few deeper cuts on his chest but nothing major.

"Manny, can you look out the window and tell me if Wayne is still out there? And, Damien, why don't you go take a shower. You're dripping mud all over my floor."

Manny made his way to the window, and Damien didn't say a word, just went to the bathroom. I sat there until I heard the shower start.

"He's not out there," Manny said looking relieved.

"What do you boys say we get ready and go outside to check over the damage from last night?"

CHAPTER 8

ONCE WE WERE ALL ready, we made our way outside moving toward the woods.

"You boys keep the cabin in view. If anything happens, you go straight back inside."

The boys nodded but didn't say anything. They just moved through the trees and looked at all the fallen branches and leaves that now scattered the forest grounds. For the most part, it didn't look like much damage happened to the grounds until I came to a batch of freshly growing sprouts and the mother tree. It was a large one with a trunk that stood the test of time. It was split in half down the middle, sagging over. As I stood there looking at it, the wind started to pick up, making a whispering sound. The earth wasn't happy with what happened here. I felt a single tear run down my face as I looked at the distraction. Taking care of the lands was something that I took such pride in that seeing the tree like this, knowing how it happened though, was what was breaking my heart.

I thought I could hear a voice off in the distance. My hearing picked up something that had the hairs on the back of my neck standing to attention. I knew whoever it was wasn't a friend. Spinning my head around, I looked to where I thought I heard the sound come from but couldn't see anything at first, so I stared harder at the spot. Was that movement, or was my mind playing tricks on me? I was fixated on that spot until I felt a hand on my shoulder, and I screamed, jumping out of my skin almost. I spun around ready to attack whatever had come up behind me only to find Damien standing there. He was freshly showered and wearing clean clothes.

"We should head back," he said, his eyes scanning the lands in a watchful manner.

"Yeah, something feels off, and I thought I heard something over there." I pointed in the direction that held my attention before the little heart attack he gave me.

Whatever was there, I knew would be gone now. Though that didn't stop me from wanting to go look but Damien stopped me.

"We should get in." He looked around the woods before he started to walk with me back toward the cabin.

"Okay, though Damien?" I couldn't keep the sound of uncertainty out of my voice.

He stopped walking and turned to look at me. "What is it, Isabel? Do you hear something?" he said as he started to look around them.

"No, it's just, well, when I was out here, I decided that tonight when the moon finally rises, I'm going to go looking for the cave."

"Isabel, we need to talk about this some more. I don't think it's a good idea for you to go wandering out there on your own right now. Besides, that dream of yours could have been more of a warning than an invitation. For all we know, one of the witches could have put the dream in your head."

We were standing next to my tree by now. Right in front of the porch, neither one of us really made a move to go into the house. The boys would be in there waiting for us to come back. This wasn't the kind of conversation they should have to hear, so I wasn't in too big of a hurry to get back inside. Given the kind of magic that was already used against us, the idea the witches could have somehow gotten into my dreams didn't seem so out of line. Though I just knew that it wasn't them. That dream meant something, and I truly had to follow it. I needed answers even though I wasn't sure on the questions. I knew this was a sign to find out the truth. A part of me was being pulled into the woods, and I knew I had to go. With the way the witches have been, I really didn't think they would care much if they killed me here or in the woods. There was nothing for them to gain from spelling me. The magics I did have were a guarded secret that I had never shown or shared with anyone other than Damien. I didn't even tell Bonnie about them, and she was my longest and best friend.

"No, it has to be tonight. There is something about tonight that I can't really explain. It's just a feeling I have deep in my bones. I have to see this, though I hope you can understand that. This is something that I must do. Please, Damien, I really hope that you can support me in this, and even if you can't, I'm still going to go and that's it. I may sound mad but there's just something in the air that I can't ignore. I have to go and see," I said, putting my head up high and walking up the steps of the porch.

"Where are you going?" asked Manny once I got inside the little entranceway.

All three of the boys had their way to listen in on anything without being detected. Though I didn't really know how to answer Manny. I couldn't even explain the idea to myself let alone Damien. I didn't think there was a way the children would understand my dream. To them, knowing the full truth of what I was thinking about doing sounded more like chasing after a nightmare than finding answers.

"I have to go out tonight and find something. Everything will be fine," I said, patting him on the back and going into the living room.

I was hoping that with that, the conversation could chance to anything else. Hoping that Damien would follow my cue and not talk about this further in front of them.

"Damien is going to stay here and watch after you guys, okay?"

"Isabel, we need to talk about this."

"No, we don't," I said as I started to pick up the now distorted living room.

"Isabel, just because you have a dream does not mean you have to go gallivanting in the woods all by yourself," he was saying as he followed me around my living room. Clearly, not following my cue of discretion.

Though one would think he would help pick up some of the mess he made, but he was too busy lecturing on the safety of the woods and how insane it would be for me to go out on my own with all the witches out there. I don't think he understood that it wasn't just a dream. I may not know what I was looking for, but I do know I needed to find it. Before I could tell him exactly where I thought he could shove his opinion, a blue orb came rushing into the room and went right up to his face.

"Why don't we go out and have a little talk?" said Zella the orb and guided him out the door.

The sight of the big bad wolf following a little blue ball around with his head down made me want to laugh, but I didn't want to lose any stance in my position of going to look for the cave, so I kept my face serious. So instead of showing my amusement, I just stared at him with a blank look in case he turned to look at me before going back out onto the porch.

A part of me knew he was only following her out of respect for me. I didn't think he would be able to take orders from anyone. Though any disrespect he would show Zella, I would be showing him the door.

Little Tommy came to stand next to me, holding pieces of the table. "Alpha Damien is about to get yelled at." He giggled.

"How do you know that?"

"Because Zella doesn't care that he's an alpha. And she thinks you should go."

Manny and Danny nodded at that.

"How do you know she thinks I should go?"

"Because she told us last night and that we shouldn't give you a hard time for it because you'll be doing it to keep us safe."

"If we give you a hard time, she said that it would make you sad because you would still have to go," Tommy said and took my hand. "It's okay."

"Well, thank you, guys. Now let's get this cleaned up. The wood pieces can go next to the firepit on the wood pile. We might as well use the wood for something productive and burn it in winter."

Damien came back inside with the orb following behind him.

The house was all picked up and I had dinner going in the oven. I figured a good dinner would put everyone a little more at ease. So I was making stuffed green peppers and au gratin potatoes and ham.

We were about to sit down when there was a knock on the door, causing me to jump, spinning around to look who was it. The shock that someone actually knocked had me jumping. Tommy's feet were running to answer the door before I got to it, though it swung open and two arguing men walked in. One was my father, Alpha Martin, and the other I hadn't actually met yet, but I knew he was Alpha William. They were followed in by three other men that I didn't recognize at all. Suddenly, my normally large enough kitchen was way too small.

Once inside though, they didn't stop arguing. Instead they started pointing fingers and acting like children, actually glancing at the three boys who were gawking at the two grown men squabbling with each other. I thought it might be an insult to compare them to the children, who were far more better behaved. Of all the ridiculous things I've ever seen, this one had to take the cake. From what I could gather, they were arguing over the witches and the proper way to proceed. Though if you were to ask me, I didn't think this method would get us anywhere. I let them argue themselves out thinking they would stop at some point and acknowledge the room, though when they didn't, I had had enough.

"Well, if this isn't a fine example of the proper way to communicate in front of children," I said, putting my hands on my hips.

It only stopped their bickering for a few minutes to glance at me, then they went right back to arguing. I just threw my hands up and gestured the boys out of their chairs and out the room.

"Come on, why don't you boys go into the living room for a bit. We don't want their goon-like behavior rubbing off onto you now, do we?"

Manny started laughing and looked at me with a twinkle in his eyes. "I could make a good goon though, Ms. Izzy."

"I'm sure you could but then I would have to send you to etiquette class now, wouldn't I?"

"What's etiquette class?" Tommy asked as little Danny started to laugh at the shocked look on Manny's face.

"Well, it's a class that will teach you boys how to be gentlemen and something that the squeaky women of the pack here teach. It's actually somewhat of a tradition for children of the pack to attend and learn how to properly behave in human society. You would learn manners and how to dance."

The face Manny made at the word dance made it clear, I would have to drag Manny kicking and screaming. Though in the long run, it would help him with his goals of alpha leadership because he would have so many different situations that it would prepare him for.

"And also, it teaches you our history and culture. It helps you learn how to be a leader. Shows you lessons learned from the history of our packs and lands." The more I thought about it, the better the idea sounded.

"Can I go?" little Tommy asked.

"Of course, all of you should go. Manny, you might actually like it and have fun. Why don't you just think about giving it a chance?"

"I'll think about it," Manny said after a few minutes of silence.

Once we got into the living room, we could hear the men still, who were arguing, clear as day.

"I swear you boys are easier to handle than the grown men that keep popping up in my home!" I said and turned, making my way back down the hallway, muttering as I went.

The boys were giggling.

Though I heard little Tommy say to the others, "I think somebody is about to get in trouble."

"I think somebody is about to get their ass kicked," Danny said back, though I didn't hear the rest of the conversation because I was already halfway down the hallway.

"Well, girly, this house seems awfully booming lately," Zella said, suddenly floating next to me.

"It certainly has been." I growled, stomping into the kitchen with the blue orb following behind me cackling.

When I got back into the kitchen, all three alphas were standing in each other's faces, just yelling at each other. Though the two men that had come in with the alphas were leaning up against the wall.

I walked right up to the three men that were just squawking at each other. "Well, I guess what they say is true," I said loud and proud, grabbing all three of their attention. "Arguing with a fool proves there are two, well, in this case three."

The two men against the wall broke out laughing.

"Isabel. Who are you calling a fool?" my father yelled, his face going red.

I could even see a vein in his forehead start to pop out.

"Right now, all of you. You all barge your way into my home just to make a ruckus of yourselves. And all three of you can stand here and argue all day, but it's not gonna get you anywhere. Now the way I see it, we can sit down and come up with a plan, or you guys can stand there and fight among yourselves while the rest of us wait for the witches to come back. Now I don't know about you three, but I got three other boys sitting in the living room counting on me to keep them safe. And I know if we let the witches win and if we let them come back to fight again, those boys are going to be in danger. So what's it going to be?" To prove my point, I pulled out a chair calmly and sat down. I folded my hands on the table in front of me and waited.

Damien was the first to sit followed by Alpha William, who was glancing at Damien from the corner of his eye. He had an odd expression on his face, though now wasn't the time to wonder about it, and to be honest, at this point, I didn't care. I was just happy he was sitting down. My father, Alpha Martin, was the last to sit. He looked so red in the face that I thought it was quite possible he was about to pop that blood vessel of a vein.

I didn't know what was coming over me before this whole mess had started. I never spoke out of turn nor did I put myself in these kinds of meetings. Now, though, watching how the men were handling things, I was starting to wonder how problems were ever sorted out in the past. These men couldn't seem to understand each other at all. It seemed like they didn't even want to try and get to an agreement. I was not going to lie. At this moment, I would settle for any mutual ground they couldn't complain about. It was like trying to coral an arm full of cats over a bucket of water. They just couldn't seem to stop hissing and spiting at each other to get anywhere in a normal conversation.

CHAPTER 9

"Now that we are all sitting down, why don't we discuss our options? In a volume that won't disturb the children. They have been through enough with everything that happened. They don't need to hear all of this as well." I gave my father a sideways glance, considering he was the loudest of all three.

One thing that I observed throughout this entire meeting was that Alpha William deferred to Damien in the arguments. Though he did it in such a sly manner that I don't think my father noticed the sideways glances. It seemed the other two men standing off to the side also looked to Damien. If I were to guess, I would think those men were actually a part of Damien's pack and not Alpha William's.

"We must take the mountain back. I say we gather up all the warriors and charge over the hills," my father declared, slamming his fist on the table making it shake. "Damien can summon all of his warriors back to the lands, which he should have already done if you ask me, and will show the witches how the mountains got their name."

"That's a foolish course of action, old man. What's to say that while we're storming the hills the witches won't be down here taking out what we leave behind? Taking control of more lands and pushing us further out," William said, and I had to admit I agreed with him—sending all the fighters up the mountain would leave us vulnerable.

"The witches are looking for something," said Damien. "There would be no point in charging an attack when we don't even know

67

what they're looking for. The first thing about good defense is that you know what you're actually defending."

"Oh yeah, boy? How do you know they're looking for something?"

My breath caught in my throat as Alpha Martin snapped at him. The tone that Martin had when he talked to Damien was not one of respect. I had heard my father talk in other alpha meetings, but I had never heard him sound so aggressive for no reason. Well, I couldn't help but wonder why he would show such outright dislike. I knew I couldn't focus on it right now. Given the way the conversation was going, my breath was stuck in my lungs. I had to count and force myself to take in much-needed air as I stared at Damien, wondering what he was going to say next.

"Why else would they suddenly want to take the mountain? We've had peace with them for centuries. They have their lands and territories. We have ours. We don't threaten their ways, and we all know witches truly have no desires in ours. There is no reason for them to come here unless they wanted something besides the peace we had with them. If they were here for some kind of help, they would have asked. No, they are here to take something they know we wouldn't just give them. The question and what's keeping me from wanting to charge right up there is what." I let go of the breath I was holding. That was a good answer and reasonable.

The fact that Damien had kept my dream to himself, I was truly grateful for him. With the mood my father was in, that bit of news would go off like a barn on fire.

"If they have no desire in our way of life and if they're happy with their amount of lands, then what could they possibly be looking for? Here we have nothing of value to the witches."

"How could you possibly know what a witch values, Father, excuse me, Alpha Martin? A witch's magic is not welcomed on our grounds. We truly don't know anything about their culture, nor do we know how to fight them. All we have are our stories from centuries ago."

"Those stories still have merit. The witches just grew confident with all the peaceful years. We defeated them once. We can defeat them again."

"We don't even know for sure how they were actually defeated before. All of our stories are different from each other's, and if you three can't agree, how are we supposed to come to a compromise?"

"Ha, a compromise. My dear, with all due respect, this is why women don't sit at a war table. You have to be able willing to fight." Alpha Martin sat back in the chair and crossed his arms.

"That's my point though. Fight how? You want to charge up the mountain and fight them head-on and then what? What's your after plan? And you"—Nodding my head to Alpha William—"you wanna set up a battlefield here in our very own backyard and wait for them to make another attack, yet you have no idea to the when, where, or how of the attack. To top it off, you can't even agree on how to prepare for the attack to come. You just want to go with the flow and hope for the best. Yes, there is no telling if the witches are going to attack here or somewhere else. Though there's also no way of knowing if the witches have planned for us to charge up the mountain and set up a counterattack. Just like Alpha William wishes to do. Though why can't we compromise on the idea and do both? Go up the mountain and stay here. Prepare for the fight to come."

"That would separate our forces," Martin said, and William nodded in agreement.

Child.

I jumped a bit at the sound of Zella as she spoke to me in my head.

Turn your chair and talk right to Damien. Tell him what you're thinking.

I took a deep breath and turned my chair, facing Damien head-on. "I have a plan," I said bluntly and with determination. "Guard the grounds and get the warriors ready for the fight. They will come back down here because they want whatever is in the cave. You stay here and fight, hold them off as best as you can. I'll go up and find the cave. Whatever is in there is what this is about, and you know it. I can find it. I know I can."

"Isabel, you're not going up there alone."

"What cave?" said Martin, and I turned and looked at him, opening my mouth to speak.

69

But the voice in my head again stopped me. *Don't tell him about your dream, child. You remember his feelings on powers,* Zella warned, and it gave me an idea.

"You remember the old story, don't you, about the two Lucan brothers who fought. They broke up the packs. One brother came down and took over flatlands. The other stayed up in the mountains. The story goes that the brother that stayed in the mountains made a cave between the lands where he left stories of the mountains whenever he missed his brother. The one that took the flatlands over, he left story in the same cave whenever he was lonely. Both were too stubborn to admit they were wrong. Until one day, the Great War broke out between the wolf and witches. It's believed that the brothers then joined together under one common enemy only to learn that they both went to the same cave. There they left whatever it was that they used to defeat them."

"That's just a children's story. You can't expect us to fight a war on a child story!" Martin yelled.

"I actually never heard about this cave. Though I know the story of the brothers. Who told you about the cave?"

"A woman whose name was Zella."

"Zella!" And there went the vein.

I truly think it finally popped. My father was going to be the first werewolf in history of our kind to fall over with a heart attack.

"The crazy old bat is the one that got this nonsense in your head. Have you lost your mind?" he screamed, standing up with the chair flying backward.

Before I could answer him though, it happened. There was a massive exploding noise off to the left of the cabin, shaking the windows and causing dishes to fall to the ground. Both alphas William and Martin shifted and charged out the door. I turned to Damien.

Go now, child, now! Zella screamed in my head, causing a force of adrenaline to course through me.

"Hold them off. Now's the time for me to go. Trust me please."

"Izzy."

The three boys were in the doorway all looking scared.

"Go to the room and close the door behind you. Stay there."

Manny grabbed the boys' arms and charged back the way he came, dragging them with him as fast as he could go.

Go, child, run. Run now.

"I must go." I ran for the door only to have Damien grab my arm and rip me back to him.

He grabbed me and kissed me as hard as he could. It got me off guard, and it took me a few minutes to respond. Just as quick as the kiss came, he let me go just as fast.

"Just be careful," he said then shifted into his own wolf and charged out the door with the two guys that I had actually forgotten were there.

Once they were out the door, I didn't wait anymore. I ran out the back door and straight for the tree line. Next to me out of the corner of my eye, I saw Zella's orb floating with me. Having her with me gave me all the strength I needed, and I pushed myself faster than I had ever ran before. Flying on my toes and soaring through the trees, I grabbed onto the branches to swing myself further and further. Ignoring the sounds of battle behind me. If I listened to it, I knew I would turn back around to help my family. I had to get there though because I knew it was our only hope.

CHAPTER 10

Z ELLA MOVED IN FRONT of me. "Stop running, child," she said.
I came to a slow stop. I rested my hands on my knees,
taking in deep breaths.

"I know the way to the caves. Rest for a minute though. I have to gather my surroundings. It's been many years. Things don't look the same."

"When were you at the cave, Zella?" I panted at her.

"When I was heartbroken by my true love. I found the cave on accident one night when I went for a run to clear my head. Though I learned a great deal when I got there." Slowly, she started moving, and I followed behind her.

I stepped over tree roots that were sticking out of the ground and climbed over large boulders. Zella floated in silence next to me as I walked. I could have sworn the woods was getting darker the further we went. It wasn't the normal kind of nighttime darkness considering there was a full moon tonight. There should have been some kind of light coming through the trees, but there wasn't any.

"Child, may I tell you a story?"

"Sure, Zella, you know I love your stories."

"Okay, well, once upon a time, there was this she-wolf that fell madly in love with her mate. She couldn't see any evil in him, though she couldn't understand why he never marked her and claimed her for his own for all to see. Though she was so in love with him, wearing his mark didn't make much difference to her. She had thought that their love was true. She had given her whole heart to him thinking that he loved her in return. Only one night, she heard a noise coming from behind some trees, a little away from where she went for a midnight run. There she found him with another woman. She was devastated and screamed running at him. She hit him, slapped him, and she yelled at him that he was her mate. She wanted to know how he could do this to her. When he answered her though, what he said had broken her heart more than what she saw. He said to her that she was too weak to be the mate of an alpha. She would never make it as a luna. The she-wolf was so devastated and turned and ran into the woods, where she stayed for weeks. When she finally emerged from hiding, she had learned that he had claimed the other woman as his mate leaving his mark on her shoulder. The scorned woman fell into great depression, and a few weeks later, she found out that she was pregnant. A few months later, she gave birth all alone to a very healthy boy. She wasn't able to raise him and had her heart broken all over again when he was taken from her right after his birth. The man's other woman raised the child as her own. Well, the true mom had to watch from the sidelines. She wanted to kick and scream and snatch her baby back, but the shame that she wasn't good enough was still stuck in her head.

"Before long, her son had grown up and was raised to think she was just the crazy lady of the pack that was missing a few screws. Eventually, her boy had his own children. Without him knowing though, one of those children started to go around the woman on her own, and she grew close to the very lonely lady. It was a relationship that gave her the chance to be the mother she knew she could be. All that heartbreak taught her a lot about life, and she passed most of those lessons on to the little girl. She didn't want the child to follow in her footsteps but make her own and make them strong and deep. One of the lessons she learned when she was getting over the heartbreak was the cave she came across. In this cave, she learned a lot about her ancestry. She learned where she really came from and the history of her bloodline."

I stopped walking and stared at her. I didn't know what to say to her about the story she just shared. The orb started to shimmer and glide around only to come flying back toward me.

"We're here, dear. Though you should probably go in first. I don't want to distract or startle you. Isabel…"

I stopped and turned to her before going to the edge. "Yes, Ms. Zella?"

"The cave isn't alone. Don't get scared, but you won't be alone in there."

"Who's in the cave?"

"The two brothers."

With that, I could feel the color run from my face. "Ms. Zella, the brothers lived centuries ago. They possibly can't still be alive."

"Oh, dear child, there is much you need to learn." She laughed and floated away. "Now down you go."

I walked to the edge of the cliff and looked over the side. As I looked, I saw how high up I was and how big of a drop it was if I lost some of my balance. I waved my arms around to balance myself. I took a deep breath and crushed down on the ground to swing my feet over the side. I just kept telling myself not to look down as I prayed to the moon goddess that my dream was true, and the ledge could fully hold my weight. I willed myself down the side of the mountain, giving my body a bit of a shimmy when I got stuck. I didn't even realize that I was holding my breath until my feet hit the ledge, and I didn't go flying down. I had my head turned to the left as I slowly wiggled across the side of the very steep mountainside. Occasionally, rocks would fall from my feet pushing off the wall. They tumbled down to whatever laid at the bottom of this gorge. I tried my best to just ignore it. At one point, I grabbed a root that was sticking out the side of the mountain, but when I put my weight on it, the root ripped out of the side, and before I knew what happened, my foot slipped. I was sliding straight down the side of the mountain.

I was grabbing frantically at anything I could get my hands on until I finally got ahold of something that stopped the descent of my body. Hitting the mountain hard, I clung there. I could feel the blood running from my hands. The dirt going into the cuts did nothing to stop the bleeding. I looked up and realized that I hadn't fallen too far from where I was, but I was defiantly going to have a bit of a climb to get back up there. I looked around me and above until my eyes caught something that looked like a larger ledge sticking out of the side of the mountain. Keeping my eyes on my goal, I just put one hand above the other and moved, slowly clawing my way up the side. I ignored the scratches and bangs my body took as I ripped through the side of the mountain. Before I knew it, the cave ledge was just one good leap away from me.

I knew I would be able to just step onto the ledge and walk in because of the angle I was coming from. So taking a deep breath, I pulled on all my strength and flung myself off the side, grabbing the edge of the ledge with a death grip. I used my claws to drag myself over the side. Once I got my chest over the side and to safety, I quickly pulled my legs up next. I laid there on my belly for a while, just catching my breath. Only the aches coming from my skin and bones got me to sit up.

There was a bright light coming from the inside of the cave just like in my dream. It looked like there was a fire going. In the light, I saw my arms and legs were shredded as blood ran down them dripping onto the ground.

"Well, now or never." I moved my legs forward one step at a time as I entered the cave.

But as soon as I stepped into the cave, a large green orb came flying at me. Just like in the dream, except this time, I didn't go flying straight backward. I turned, putting my back against the cave wall.

"We have company!" the orb boomed in a deep voice.

"I see that," growled a different voice coming from the side.

I looked over to see a red orb slowly floating over. The red orb then said something that wasn't in English, and the green orb answered. There I stood watching, as it seemed, two random orbs arguing with each other. Then to add into the insanity, in floated my orb. The blue of Zella's orb shone brighter and brighter the closer she got to them.

"Is this any way to act when you finally have someone here to see you?" she bellowed at the two of them.

I could have sworn the other two orbs turned to looked at her.

"Why, Zella, is that you?" said Mr. Green.

"It's been ages, my dear. And who do we have here?" said Mr. Red, flying right up to me to get a good look at me. "Oh, let me guess. Long brown hair, pretty blue eyes."

"Deep blue, almost like the sea," Mr. Green cut in.

"Yes, brother, a deep blue, and you smell that."

"It's faint and washed out, but I sense Lucan. It's been faded though."

"Yes, I believe what we have here is little baby Isabel."

"I do believe you're right."

I just kept turning my head to look at the orb that was speaking until I realized it was my turn to speak. "Um, hello. Yes, I'm Isabel and you guys would be the two brothers?" I was so beyond confused.

"Yes. I'm Arthur and this would be my brother, Henry," said the green orb.

"What can we do for you?" said Henry, the red orb.

"Well…I don't really know. You see, the witches broke the peace and attacked the mountains. The mountain fell to them for the main warriors were gone, and the witches timed it out just right. I had a dream that told me to come here, so here I am."

"You're telling us…" said Henry the red.

"You swung the mountainside?" came from Arthur's, the green orb.

Both of them were moving around me, and I was having a hard time keeping them straight. Though I didn't move and kept looking straight ahead at Zella because she was standing constantly right across from me on the other side of the cave.

"Because you had a dream?" Henry again.

"Well, yeah. You see, I had a dream after the pack lands and mountains were attacked. In the dream, I came here for some kind of answers as to how we can win against this magic against us. The woman that raised me, she bereaved in the powers of the land spirits and thought that the mountains held all the secrets to our past and future. I'm only here because I want to save my people from the witches' fire. There is something wrong with the magic they are using. We don't know how to fight it. I also think the reason the witches attacked the mountains first wasn't because the strongest warriors lived there, but because of something that is hidden here. Though I have no idea what that could be. Going by the kind of powers they're using though, I think it would be really bad it they find whatever it is first."

"You think the witches attacked for the something?" Arthur said.

"Brother, are you thinking what I'm thinking?" Henry said and moved away from us.

"It's possible."

"Maybe it's time too."

"I think you're right."

"What's possible and time to do what? I just came here in hopes of answers as what to do."

"Why are you the one that came?" Arthur asked.

I thought there was something off about his tone, like he was deep in thought.

"Because the men were too busy arguing with each other, and a wise woman always said that if you want something done right, you have to do it yourself. Magic is not allowed in the pack lands, and they wouldn't support this idea of a course of action."

"So you're here without the alpha support or knowledge?"

"Yes, I am here without my alpha's knowledge. Though another alpha knows I'm here and why. I told him about my dream, and he thought along the same lines that I did. He thought that it was a sign that something worse was going to come if we didn't do something now. The witches were in the process of hitting my pack's lands when I started out to get here. For all I know, it's already too late, and there is nothing to do to stop what's clearly coming. The packs aren't prepared. Some don't even know the battle came because the ones that run it were too busy arguing with each other to come to any course of action. Does this answer your question?"

"Yes, yes, I believe it does."

Then Henry and Arthur started talking to each other in whatever language they were speaking. I stood there waiting, and I looked back at Zella. I think she was calm because she wasn't overly bright or shimmering. Just a steady crystal blue. Now that I sat there, I wondered why there were three different orbs. I couldn't help but be curious why they were different colors. If I lived through all of this, I will have to ask. As the men talked it over, I watched them, and they didn't seem to be hating each other. If I had to guess I would say they were talking about the best course of action to handle this news.

The excitement of this adventure was really kicking in as I got tired. I moved back against the wall and slid down to sit on the dirt to rest for a few minutes before the two came back.

"We've come to a decision. We have decided that we will give you the book that you are looking for. It holds spells of the old world, and you must protect it at all costs for if this book falls into the wrong hands, it could lead to a devastating effect on our kind."

"And we have decided to gift you with our small library if you wish to take it."

"We think it's time to pass down our stories, and we think you will have respect and understanding for what you read."

"Hopefully, it will give you guidance in your future journeys."

"Follow us please."

Together, we went further into the cave. When we got further in the cave, the orbs turned and went don't a narrow hallway. I shimmed down behind them. It opened into a smaller room with a stream of water coming from somewhere.

"Take these books. They are all yours," said Arthur, and I went over sliding my backpack off and slid the three very large books into it.

"Thank you. I'll take good care of them. I swear."

"We wish to come back with you."

"We've been in these caves for a very long time and an outing would be good for us."

"Your more than welcome to stay with me and Zella, though I'm not sure what we're going back to."

"That's why we want to go. This is going to be a good show."

"A little excitement after so long will be good for us."

"Even though we are spirits, we still have a few tricks. Let's give these witches something to think long and hard about."

"Besides, for as long as I'm around, my mountain will not fall." This was said with a growl as the red shimmer around him burned hard, casting a hue over the whole room.

"There is another way out of here. Follow us," said Arthur, and he moved down a different tunnel.

For this one, I had to crawl on my hands and knees to make it there, at some points army crawl. When I came to the end of the tunnel, the fresh air slammed into my face welcoming me to the exit. I took a deep breath of freedom.

Chapter 11

" I HAVE A FUN fact for you, child," said Henry as his orb swayed from side to side. "Did you know that when trees first started to grow on this earth that their roots couldn't plant themselves into the ground. So the trees would grow big, but they'd fall over because the root system couldn't hold them up over time. When the trees started to decompose into the earth though, the trees made the ground strong. In doing so, it made the future trees stronger and taller. The new trees' roots became firmly planted into the ground. It's believed that it took sixty million for the trees to become fully established," Henry said as we made our way through the woods.

"Really?" I asked, surprised at this.

"Yes," Henry said, his orb bobbing up and down.

We walked a little further in silence.

"Not to sound rude but what does that have to do with any of what's going on now?"

"Think about it my, dear. It's about how you are going to defeat the witches. They are using magic that you may never have seen or known about. That doesn't mean your ancestors haven't seen it though. Like the tree roots, you need your bloodline to become stronger in spirit and in battle."

"I must ask, why are you guys, umm, orbs? Excuse me if this sounds rude, but why aren't you resting?"

"Well, you see, I fell in battle with the vampires," Henry said, and I spun around to stare at him in shock.

"Vampires? They're real?"

"Very real, yes. Though they don't really like to be disturbed. They keep to themselves. You see, the daughter of the vampire king had fallen in love with a werewolf. Her father was livid and assembled an army to collect her. Though the wolf was her true mate, all the packs of the flatland, as you call them, gathered together to fight them. We lost many but so did they."

When he stopped talking, I came to a stop not even realizing I wasn't moving until all three orbs turned to look at me.

"How did it end?"

"I'm not sure, to be honest. I was kind of dead," Henry said, laughing though I didn't see the humor in it.

"I know how it ended," Arthur said quietly.

"How?"

We started moving again, weaving through trees. The sun was starting to come through the trunks.

"I was up in the mountains when a messenger came up to see me. My brother had sent a messenger to give me update on his life and about things that happened below. I see now that it was his attempt to reach out and repair our relationship. Back then though, I saw it as bragging and sent every message back with nothing in return. This messenger though…" Arthur stopped for a moment as if gathering his thoughts. "He approached me as I was sitting high on my throne and fell to his knees. He told me about the war and that my brother had fallen. The rage that had coursed through me was something that I had never felt before. I sent every warrior the mountain had down with the order to kill every one of them. Well, the flatlands had been hoping to come to an understanding and compromise. The mountains didn't want compromise. We wanted dust in our teeth and claws."

"That's when the mountains woke up?" I whispered, remembering the story I heard as a child. "The day the mountain woke was the day thunder rained down on the lands below, shaking the world beneath our feet. Something to be feared as the fires of hell consumed everything below."

"Yes. You see, the grief I felt was so great. A grief because of all the time I wasted being angry simply due to the fact that my brother found love with a human. We had relations then with the witches. Relations is the wrong word. It was more like an understanding. The witches hated the vampires and happy to join us in the fight. The battle lasted for three nights, and the vampires fell at the full force of the anger that came down around them. Then the vampire king finally understood that his daughter refused to reconsider her love. It took her facing him at the center of the field. She was something to behold in a fight, almost danced around the field with such grace. After it was all over with, she turned her mate. If I remember right, I think they are still alive and well. Right, brother?"

"I, well, umm…" Henry was clearly confused. "Yes, they are. We should send them a message. See if they will join us in the fight. I didn't realize what my passing caused."

"Yes. Well, now you know, and we should focus on the matter at hand," Arthur said uncomfortably.

"Of course. We are orbs because we had unfinished business. The moon goddess seeing this gave me a choice. She asked me if I was ready, and I wasn't," Henry said.

"Me as well. I passed naturally though. After the battle, I wasn't the same. I retreated back to the mountains, though I kept an eye on the lands in memory of my brother. When it was my time, I couldn't leave my brother's lands unwatched."

"So then you two met each other in the afterlife?"

"Well, yes actually. We both went to the cave after our passing, and that was where we met," Henry said.

"It was a good laugh after we finished yelling at each other for a year or two," Author said.

"You mean after everything, when you finally saw each other again, you spent years still arguing?"

"Yes," both of them said, and I just shook my head at them.

We were about a mile from the tree line for my cabin.

"Zella, what was your unfinished business?"

"Now, child, where would the fun be in telling you?" Zella laughed, though she became silent as the atmosphere changed.

The air became electric, and the memory of the attack that had come the night before rushed to my mind.

"We have company."

With that ordering, howls went up into the air. They sounded so ferocious you could feel it vibrating in your chest. As we approached closer to the tree line, there had to be about thirty wolves that came charging, surrounding us. They were snarling with their teeth bared. Coming through the pack was a large black wolf. As he approached, he shifted, and I let out the deep breath I was holding because it was Damien.

"Took you long enough," he said, coming to stand in front of us. "Come on, the trees aren't safe. They seem to have a mind of their own." With that, Damien looked at the trees, and for the first time since I met him, I saw true fear in his eyes.

"Missed you too. You try finding the caves. It wasn't an easy journey."

"I see that. Are you all right?" He looked me up and down, which reminded me that I was covered in dried blood, dirt, and who knew what else.

"Nothing that a tub can't fix. Now what did you do to upset my trees?"

As soon as the words "my trees" left my mouth though, all the wolves, except Damien's, heads snapped up and they all turned tail and sprinted back the way they came. Damien gave me a side-eye as they walked out of the trees. That's when I saw all the damage from the fight before. Everything looked like a wrecking ball came through here; smaller trees were knocked over, and there were crater-sized holes everywhere. Thankfully though, all the homes looked relatively undamaged.

"Wow, this all happened last night?" I knew the battle was going to be bad, but this hurt my heart. The destruction was all around.

As they got closer, I could see people moving around and picking things up and making repairs. Approaching the cabin, the door swung open and out ran the three boys, who charged down the stairs shoving each other out of the way. They got to me with such force that knocked me over onto the ground, tackling me. All three of them were talking at once and so fast that I was missing more of what they were saying.

Damien reached down and lifted them off. "Let's all just get inside. You can get cleaned up and then we'll figure out what our next steps will be. They is going to be a war meeting in a little bit to go over plans."

"Good. I haven't run a war conference in centuries," Arthur said and floated ahead of us into the house.

"Brother, does this mean you have a plan?" Henry said, going after him, and I could hear Arthur laughing.

"Of course I do. Now we must prepare for the conference."

Damien was staring at me. "I see you made friends on your trip."

"Yes, umm, meet the brothers." Walking into the cabin, I lifted my hands to the orbs, first to the green orb. "This is Arthur, the brother from the mountains, and this"—I moved to gesture to the red orb—"this is Henry of the flatlands."

"You mean the brothers, brothers?"

"Yes, well, I'm going to take a quick tub and go over the books. Well, you guys get to know each other." And with that, I fled down the hall, suddenly really needing to get this mess out of my hair and off my skin.

The books were getting heavier as I stood in the living room. If this was what the witches were after, then there has to be something useful in them.

As I made my way, I could hear Damien talking to the orbs. It sounded civil and respectful. It was surprising how well he was handling the whole magic and orbs situation considering it was truly weird even for our kind. He acted like they were human still and gave them the respect their past deserved.

Running a tub and letting the water fill it, I pulled one of the books out and started to skim and read through it. When I finally sunk down into the water, I felt all my muscles loosen up and relax. I soaked and thought about what to do next.

CHAPTER 12

WHEN I FINALLY EMERGED from the bedroom fully dressed and with a decent idea of a plan of attack, I felt more put together only to come into the living room to find it full. There was more arguing going on, though, than planning. I truly didn't know how three alphas, three orbs, three boys sitting in the corner, and five warriors leaning up against the walls could all fit in such a tiny room. All I seem to be missing in the space was a partridge in a pear tree. The orbs were just floating around silently as everyone else yelled like children. Funny thing was, the actual children in the room were sitting quietly, just watching the ridiculousness. Considering I hadn't slept in what felt like forever and we didn't know when the witches were gonna come back, this didn't seem very proactive. Also, not something I seemed to have the patience for at the moment. I will never understand why men cannot seem to get along. Is talking out a solution that hard for their species?

"Enough of this. All of you are behaving like children, and considering I got three children that are better behaved, I feel that's an insult to them. I was only soaking for a half hour. How all of you can already be at your throats seems a little ridiculous to me."

"My dear, it was just getting good," Zella said, floating next to me.

"Really? Because it sounded like it was getting nowhere." I turned to Damien and the brothers who were standing off to the side together. "I have an idea. I have been thinking of a plan, and I came up with something."

"We have also been thinking and have come up with something," Arthur finally spoke from the spot he was floating on. "I was going to share but it's been so long since I watched some alphas throw their testosterone around. I was wondering who was going to win. Though my money would be on the boy. There's something about his eyes."

"Well, that's nice," I said exasperated with all this. "Would you like to go first? We really need to get an idea on how we want to handle this," I asked Arthur since he was an expert in the subject. I took in a deep breath, holding it for a few minutes before slowly letting it out.

"Now wait just a minute. Give me one good reason why I should be listening to a shining talking ball," boomed Martin. His voice vibrating off the walls around us.

"Because that shining talking ball is Lord Arthur of the mountains. You know, from the legion. Also, he's seen this kind of magic before. It's good to learn from our history, Martin."

"Now, Isabel, I have let you entertain the ideas of that crazy old bat for long enough. I thought after she passed, the effect she had on you would eventually fade, but seeing as the woman has figured out a way to come back and haunt me, we need to start thinking more logically on how to proceed."

"Well, you know, after some deep thought, I think I rather like my grandmother's way better, and it gave me an idea on how to win this. Before you even start, yes, the crazy old bat is my grandma. This isn't the time to be holding onto old anger. We have to get past this. Please if the both of you will just hear us out, maybe, just maybe, we can defeat the witches and win the mountain back. Then we can all move on with our lives. Or you two can keep arguing with each other, bringing up old issues that have nothing to do with this moment, and we can lose because there is no solid plan. And we're divided."

"A woman does not belong talking about war plans," Martin said.

"Well, I for one so far have liked all of Isabella's ideas, and I agree with the brothers' plan of action. Given the fact that I hold the actual weight of the warriors of the mountains, I think we should hear Isabel out," Damien cut in, pushing himself off the wall. It would seem even Damien had enough with this as well.

"Yeah, I've heard about your liking of Isabel from Wayne. Makes me wonder if you like her ideas or if you just want to get close to her. Without a mating mark."

The mating mark was more like a wedding ring among our kind, and I couldn't help but think that it was a low blow. My back straightened at the insult, though I didn't know if it was an insult at me or Damien.

Before I could say anything though, Damien was in Martin's face and, with a low voice, said to him exactly what he thought, though it showed I defiantly missed something, "Considering your plan last night could have gotten most of your men killed, I would think better of insulting those that have kept us alive. I think living here so peacefully without much challenge has made you too comfortable."

"Now listen here, boy—" Martin bellowed, but Damien laughed at him, cutting him off.

"Without the weight of the mountains, you will fall. Fact. Without me or my men, you would have lost last night. And lastly without whatever's Ms. Zella's and Isabel's trees did last night, we would have all lost. We didn't stand a chance at what came from the woods and you know it."

"What exactly did happen last night?" I asked, truly feeling like I missed some great story.

"I can tell you about it later. We have more pressing issues to discuss. Why don't you tell us about your trip into the woods? Did you find anything that could help?"

So I told them the story about finding the caves and getting to the caves. I thought they were going to blow a gasket when I told them about my falling and climbing my way back up. Clearly, they were not disliking what I had done. Though whether they were liking it because of the risk I took or the fact that I went alone, I didn't know. They were complaining about both facts. When I got to the books and was telling them what I found inside them, I told them about my plan.

In the book, there was this resurrecting the sprits spell. When I was flipping through the pages, it all but jumped off the pages to me. If I understood the old writings correctly, you can use the spell as a calling to the spirits long since passed to ask them for guidance or help. Hearing the story about the fight with the vampires gave me the idea. What if we could call the old warriors of both the flatlands and the mountains to fight together for one last battle?

At some point through my story and idea, between the part of me falling off the side of the mountain and calling the spirits to join in arms, Martin had had enough of my, as he called it, crazy ramblings. He had turned to Zella and blamed her for the runaway thoughts that she had put into my head. He announced that he was going to prep his warriors for battle and would see us on the field when the time came. As he was leaving, he was muttering about the crazy old bat the whole way out the door. Though I had to admit, muttering to himself that way, he seemed to be the crazy one. When the door slammed behind him, I had to say I felt a sense of relief. If he had that big of a problem with attacking trees, he really wasn't going to like or support my other ideas. They all required magics of some sort or another.

"Well, now that the close-minded fool is gone," said William, clearly content with Martin's leaving as well. "Now you were telling us about some summing things you found?"

"Yeah, well, in theory, you can call and ask for help from warriors past. They don't have to come and can choose to ignore it. To be honest though, I'm not sure what help they can give us. They won't be able to fight."

"We may not be able to fight tooth and claw, but that doesn't mean we don't have some tricks up our sleeves. Never underestimate those who have been around longer than the time of our stories."

"Yes, the stories of our kind were built off the men that you want to call."

"Don't forget, child, magic wasn't always so discouraged among our kind either. Something that some people have forgotten is it takes magic for us to shift into our wolf forms. Our kind used to respect it in a way that has slowly went out of style."

"Zella is right. Some packs still have seers but not all. Slowly, it seems like the gift is being bred out and not passed to generations."

"I don't think it's being bred out. I think it's becoming ignored," William said. "I have spent more time with Martin than I ever thought I would have to, and I have to say if I had the gift, I would pretend I didn't too," William said, looking at me.

"What do you mean too?" Damien said.

I got a sick feeling in my stomach suddenly.

"Ah, because little Isabel here has the gift. She got it from Zella of course."

"I don't have any gifts."

"Child, you do. You just don't see it yet. That's why the trees respond to you, and you understood my spells even as a little pup. Your sister doesn't have the gift. I can promise you that. Sometimes I wonder about that girl."

"I think maybe it would be hard to understand that you have a special gift if gifts are considered outlawed," Henry said, coming around to float around me. "One day, you will see what you can do."

"I have a feeling that when the day comes, it will be more historic than when the mountains thundered," Arthur said with a laugh at this.

"I think we need to get back to the point at hand. I can't read this spell, and I don't even know who I would be contacting."

"Let me see it," Zella said, coming to float next to me.

"I'm thinking if you can read it and since its Arthur's and Henry's warriors we are trying to call, if the three of you did it together, we would have a better outcome."

"This is a good idea, and it would be worth a shot. That is if my brother is okay with this idea. We all know he's a little finicky with war plans," Henry said with a laugh.

"I have never had a problem with magic. I'm not sure why it became so frowned upon. I think it's a good idea and worth a try. Now what about the warriors? What's the plan with them?" Arthur said, and if he was in human form, I could have sworn he would be rubbing his hands together in glee.

I never would have thought someone would be so excited for a battle. Arthur seemed so at ease with the subject it made me wonder what times back then were truly like.

"I have a plan for that," said Damien as he turned the guys that were once again standing against the wall silently. "Doc, you're up." He was stepping off to the side when I looked confused. "Doc is my second-in-command," he said in clarification.

With that, we hashed out the rest of the defense.

CHAPTER 13

PICKING UP AFTER THE meeting, I had just gotten the living room mostly back to normal when there was a knock on the door. I didn't want to think about the fact that I got excited, hoping it was Damien. Maybe he forgot something and decided to return. Though I knew it was silly because he had yet to knock. Also silly because there was no reason for me to be excited at the idea of him stopping back over. Every time I saw him, I felt this pull to him that was growing. My brain thought better when he wasn't around, but ever since the meeting ended, I couldn't get the thought of him out of my mind. Though any excitement I may have felt faded just as fast when I saw it was Wayne.

"Wayne, what do you want?"

"I'm gathering wood for the annual fire. It's right around the corner, you know? I was wondering if you had some you wanted to spare?"

"We're still having the fire? Don't you think that's rather silly with everything that is going on?"

"Well, a distraction is good, and besides the guys from up high don't seem to be really understanding the way we do things. It would be good to show them some of our culture, don't you think?"

"I think it would be rather difficult to try and change their way of doing things. Besides, with no one really knowing what the witches are going to do next, maybe it wouldn't be a good idea to give them a beacon right for us."

"Isabel, there's no need to be scared. I'll be there. I can look after you."

"Well, I won't be going this year. Not with everything going on. Besides, I don't want to leave the boys home alone and don't think they're ready for that kind of outing yet. This is a lot for them to take in."

"The boys? Are you still stuck with those mountain runts?"

"Excuse me?"

"Isabel, why don't you just give the children back to the women that are taking care of the rest of them? You don't want them getting attached to you. Besides, this fire is a big deal. It's the start of the mating dance."

"Well, Wayne, I'm more than happy if the children get attached to me. I like having them here. And since this is my cabin, I think I'm able to have whoever I want here."

"I mean no disrespect about the little squirts. I'm just saying you're young yet. Why set yourself with pups so close to the mating dance? How would you explain them to any male that was interested in you?"

"Wayne, this may come as a surprise to you, but not all women are jumping at the idea of getting mated to some ground-thumping, chest-bumping *Neanderthal* that's denser than a pile of rocks. Well, that may float some girls' boats. I think the weight of your ego may sink mine. Have a good day now." With that, I closed the door in his face and turned around only to be staring at none other than Damien.

He was leaning up against the wall, out of view from the doorway. His expression was blank on his face. He just leaned there with his arms crossed, staring at me.

"Can I help you?" I was suddenly not so happy to see him. Why was it I only saw him at embarrassing moments?

"Well, I was going to ask what's for dinner, but now I'm thinking that's a bad idea. You want to go out to eat? We can gather up the boys and head to that diner downtown."

"That sounds good actually because I haven't even gotten around to what I was going to make them for dinner."

I was just about to yell for the boys when they came walking down the hallway, all ready to go.

"You boys ready?"

"Damien, where are you taking us?" Tommy asked, really excited. He was doing his happy bounce that he seemed to do whenever he was looking forward to something.

"Down to the diner for dinner," Damien said to him and patted Tommy's head.

"I like Isabel's cooking though," said Manny.

Manny didn't seem as excited about the idea of going out as Tommy was. I looked at Danny wondering what kind of reaction he had. Though he seemed rather indifferent to the idea, I really did find it fascinating how different these three boys were, but they always got along so well. Despite being so young, they reminded me of a functional unit, always evening each other out.

"Yeah, well, she could probably use a night off. Besides, you guys like eating out," Damien said with a laugh.

"Yeah, but Isabel can cook."

"Thanks, kid."

With that, we all made our way to the car. Well, the boys talked about their day's excitement and garden herbs. The whole time, Damien just sat there smiling. He was driving further into town. I thought it was odd driving there because I walked everywhere, except during winter. Sometimes the snow got so heavy here that even driving through it had issues.

Once we got to the diner, the boys wrestled themselves out of the car, tumbling to the ground. On the way in, I saw Bonnie and waved her over.

"Well, hello there, sunshine!" I yelled out to her.

It felt like years since I last saw her, though I knew it was only days. This had to be the longest week I have ever had. The idea that everything had changed for me in such a little bit of time made my head spin. The funny thing about this whole thing was that I couldn't really remember what it was like before I had the boys and all of this drama around me. How quickly you can get used to disaster was something remarkable if you really took a few minutes to think about it.

"Hey, what are you doing here?" Bonnie said, coming over by us.

"Damien figured we'd go out to eat tonight. A good outing for the boys, you know, add a little excitement to an already exciting life." I laughed and gave her a quick hug. I turned and introduced her to the guys. "This is Damien, and I'm sure you probably met the boys, Manny, Danny, and Tommy. They have been staying with me."

Tommy came up to my side and wrapped his arms around my legs.

"That makes sense. It's nice to meet you, Damien, boys."

"Who are you here with?"

"No one. I just finished my shift at the clinic, and I was hungry."

"Why don't you join us? Tommy, you remember me telling you about my friend that knows more about medicine than I do, right?"

"Yeah," he said shyly behind my legs.

"Well, this is her. Bonnie is my best friend and an amazing doctor. She's the reason I planted most of those herbs in the yard." Then I looked up at Bonnie. "Eat with us?"

"Sure, why not."

Together, we all made our way into the diner and to a booth. The boys slid in first.

"Well, Bonnie, how do you like being a doctor?"

"I enjoy it a lot. I like the mystery of medicine. I'm working on learning nature herbs now. Even gone to study with witch doctors."

"I have a guy in my pack that does all our patching up. We call him Doc but doesn't really go to classes to learn stuff like that. He mostly does patchwork."

"Like the scar?" Then she froze realizing how that sounded. "What I mean, well, I'm sorry."

"It's okay." Damien started laughing. "Yeah, like the star. Not too bad of a job considering we were in the middle of a battle many years ago. One of the first ones that we had to fight." Damien seemed to drift off into thought as he spoke. "A pack of rogue wolves attacked a small village that we were just passing through. It was just the two of us then. We weren't as experienced then. Just out of training really. The two of us decided to go on an adventure through the flatlands.

When the rogues attacked, no one saw it coming. One of them got me around the throat. We were trapped down in some bushes, and he had to close it to stop the bleeding." Suddenly, he started to laugh. "That's how he got the name Doc actually."

"That's a story." Bonnie laughed. "I hope I didn't offend you."

"Not at all, it's fine. Why don't you tell me about herself?"

At this point, our food came and we all started eating.

Bonnie looked at me uncertain. "I don't know."

"Bonnie doesn't really like to talk about herself. That's why she's so good at studying medicine. Bonnie sweetie, why don't you tell him about your sisters."

"Oh well, I got two younger sisters. They're twins. They couldn't be even more different though. They are away at college. Mary is going for an English major with a minor in history and the youngest of the twins. Malloy, well, she, umm, she can't really make up her mind and is studying this and that. Personally I thought she should have just waited to go. Malloy is more of a party happy girl. Well, Mary keeps to herself. The funny thing is they are both cheerleaders. Go figure."

"We always joked that the only reason Mary got stuck cheerleading was because of Malloy. You see, Bonnie's parents are a little bit strict."

"You see, it was funny because, well, Mary is one of the best cheerleaders and almost got a full scholarship because of cheerleading and her test scores. She absolutely hates to be the center of attention. She will do anything to just float around without drawing notice to her."

"Though Malloy, on the other hand, loves attention. She's good at cheerleading too, but the fun is what she cares about."

"Malloy is very live for the moment." Bonnie laughed, and we continued to talk through the meal about medicine and how the people in the hospital were doing.

Damien told us funny stories from up in the mountains. It was nice to learn these things about the people that were now all around us. Listening to him talk, I could have sworn I had known Doc for years. The boys were adding their one-liners. It was one of the best nights I had in a very long time. When the bill came, Damien didn't let either one of us pay. I almost laughed at the look on Bonnie's face. I think if it was physically possible, she would have swallowed her own tongue. Though to his credit, he didn't show that he noticed her floundering about.

CHAPTER 14

WHEN DAMIEN FINALLY TURNED down the road, Tommy was fast asleep in the back seat leaning up against Danny. Danny was simply looking out the window with complete ease. When we finally parked, Damien got out to open the back door and lifted Tommy out of the car. Manny was the first one to run inside. I knew he was running in there to get to the book he was reading. I didn't want to let on that I knew he was enjoying the story line of pirates. It was one of my childhood favorites. I stayed on the porch for a little bit. I needed to clear my head from all the noise of the day. A few deep breaths of clean air would make everything good as new.

As I stood there though, I thought I heard something just off to the side of the house. Spinning my head in the direction, I stared as hard as I could. I knew I heard something, though, a part of me was starting to feel as paranoid as Ms. Zella. I was about to cast the trick on the trees when the deer poked its head out from the bushes. I started to laugh a bit at my own reaction. Shaking my head, I went inside and almost ran into Damien.

"What are you smiling at?"

"I just had the daylights scared out of me by a deer of all things," I said, still giggling.

"Well, that's one way to end the day. I was thinking I'm going to head back into town and get a treat for us. I'll be back in a little bit."

"Oh, okay."

"Don't worry, I told the boys too. They want to stay up to read. Read? What did you do to those boys?"

"I don't have a TV, remember? It took a bit to get the boys to come around, but I think they are starting to like it."

Damien just started to laugh, shaking his head as he made his way out the door, probably passing the deer on his way back to the car. So I headed into the living room to find the boys already settled onto the couch. Manny and Danny were deep into reading their books while Tommy was sleeping off to the side of them. I grabbed my own and settled into the recliner. It was nice how content we could just be.

As I was relaxing, I started to drift off only to wake up when Tommy came over to climb into my lap, settling in and started to drift back to sleep. It wasn't until there was a knock at the door that woke the room up. Thinking it was Damien coming back with the treat, I nodded to Manny to go get the door.

"Why are you here?" I heard Manny say.

"Is Isabel home, kid?" I heard Wayne answer, and I couldn't help but roll my eyes at the sound of his voice.

We were having such a nice night. It was quiet and relaxing, something the boys and I needed. If I thought it was Wayne, I wouldn't have let Manny answer the door. The kid had a short fuse, and the more Wayne hung around here, the more I didn't want him by the children. So I slowly moved Tommy off me because I didn't want to wake him. Getting to my feet, I heard Manny talking, making me freeze in my spot.

"I heard you before, you know? You don't want us here. That's okay though because Isabel doesn't want you here and neither do we."

"What did you just say to me, boy?"

"Go away! She doesn't want to see you!"

"You need to learn your place," Wayne snarled, and it was the kick I needed to get moving.

Before I could get to the door though, Manny's temper snapped, and I saw him punch Wayne in the stomach.

"Manny, no!" I moved to grab his arm and moved him out of the way from Wayne.

Out of the corner of my eye, I saw Wayne starting to sprout fur, a snarl coming over his face. Seeing him start to change on my porch, I just reacted without thinking. I threw Manny behind me and grabbed the fire extinguisher that was right next to the front door in case something went wrong with the fireplace. Wayne had finished his shift and was getting ready to pounce, rearing his back end up in the air while snarling his teeth at me. I pulled the pin of the fire extinguisher and pointed it straight at him, pulling the trigger. Cold white foam shot out the end of the nozzle in a messy cloud. Wayne fell backward at the shock, rolling down the steps and hitting the ground. I followed him out, still spraying him down with the white foam until it ran out. Then I rushed back in, slammed the door shut, and locked it. I put my back against the door and looked down at Manny, who had his mouth gaped.

"You sprayed him with a fire extinguisher?"

"Yes."

"You can't spray people with fire extinguishers."

I smiled at him, remembering our talk from the other night. "Well, I did."

"Yes, you did." And then Manny bust out laughing.

I looked up from Manny to see Damien coming down the hallway from the kitchen. Remembering the back door was unlocked, I bolted from leaning on the door, sprinting to the kitchen to grab the lock on the door.

"What!" I heard Damien yell from the other room.

I had to raise my eyes to the ceiling. I took a deep breath and asked the moon goddess for the strength to deal with these men who have taken over my life. Moving out of the kitchen, I went back to the living room and was treated with an innocent-looking Manny. He was standing there with his hands folded in front of him and looking up at me with his big brown eyes. Damien was nowhere to be seen though. I was about to ask him where Damien had gone when the front door was opened, and he walked in.

"He's gone!" Damien growled, clearly unhappy.

"Yes. Everything is fine, Damien, don't worry."

"I think it may be time for me to have a talk with Wayne. He seems to not be understanding what it means for a woman not to be interested in him."

"Wayne just has a big head. I think he got his point, though, when he got a face full of foam." I laughed, walking up to Damien to put my hand on his back. "I don't think he will be coming back here anytime soon. Don't worry about it. This is something that I can take care of. I promise everything will be fine. Now what treat did you bring?" I changed the subject as Danny and Tommy joined us in the hallway.

Damien saw them coming and forced a smile on his face as he looked at the two boys. Manny kept that innocent look on his face which was really unnerving. I think I liked it better when he was glaring at everything. For some reason, when he looked innocent like a child, it reminded me of someone who was up to no good. I could almost see the wheels turning in his mind.

"I got everyone some ice cream orange floats. Come on, I set them down in the kitchen." Damien started to herd the boys toward the kitchen.

Tommy took off running toward the promise of ice cream. The boys attacked the drinks with a savage intensity that I couldn't help but laugh at.

After the boys finished the drinks, I sent them off to bed ready to bring this day to the end. Once I tucked them in, I came back into the living room to find Damien sitting on the couch, looking perfectly at home. I moved to sit next to him.

"Tonight was very nice. Thank you for taking us out and for the floats. The boys were clearly very happy with that. It's nice to see them so excited."

"They like you."

"I like them. I like having them here. They bring live to this cabin."

"They are good at that." He laughed. "You have to stay on your feet with those three." Damien's hand moved to the back of my neck and started to play with my hair.

When I looked at him, I couldn't help it...I leaned over and kissed him. Before I could really wrap my head around it, we were sitting on the couch and tugging at each other's clothes. Eventually moving toward the bedroom and shutting the door.

CHAPTER 15

WAKING UP TO THE cabin shaking, I shot up in bed. Damien was moving around the room, getting dressed and talking on the phone. He was calling the warriors into action. The witches were here. There was no time to think. I got up and threw on some sweats, running out of the room to get to the boys. I found them already in the hidden room sitting together on the floor with the blue orb of Zella floating over them.

"About time you were up, girl."

"Zella, the witches are here."

"Clearly. Now what are you waiting for, child?"

A book flipped open on the table to the page that called the spirits of those passed as Arthur and Henry came into the room.

"Well, will you look at that," Arthur said, though I found it very concerning how outright giddy he sounded. "The sounds of batter are marvelous on such a beautiful morning."

"I'm really starting to think there is something wrong with your head, Arthur," I said, laughing at him.

It was truly deranged how happy a fight made this man. The fact that someone got so much enjoyment out of moments like this was not something I could understand.

"Look, there are many different ways to look at this moment. You can look at it as a battle with fear, or you can look at it as the ending to this whole event," Henry said in a calming manner, clearly at peace in this moment. "Now start reciting. We have old friends to call."

I knelt down on the floor and started to say the old words that would call to the fallen. Zella's voice mixing in with mine as an acting beckon.

"To those passed that sound and claimed the mountains. To those passed that stood and claimed the flatlands. We call upon you. Answer the call of your alphas one last. We call upon to aid and hear us. Call upon the fallen. Moon Goddess, heed our call for wish to speak with the men of the lost times."

The air in the little room started to spin around us. It was like bringing in the middle of a tornado. I looked over at the boys and saw Manny had his arms around Danny and Tommy protectively, though none of them looked scared as they watched the air move faster and faster. Suddenly, balls of lights of all different colors started to spin around us.

Arthur moved to the center of the room. His voice was booming off the walls as he started his battle speech. "Men, we want to ask you to fight one last time. You gave your lives for the lands and our freedoms already. Making the great sacrifice and joining the moon goddess in all her glory. That's why I'm asking for your help. Not as your alpha but as someone that needs your help. We cannot stand without the strength of the great wolves that build what we have. I'm asking for you to choose to stand with me one last time, one last battle. Stand with me and my brother and fight," Arthur said as William came up to float next to him.

"Without you, the witches are too strong. If you choose to decide to join us in battle, we understand and thank you for your past loyalty to your pack lands and wish you nothing by a restful peace. Though we hope that you will stand and fight not because you have to but because you want to."

"We wouldn't be disturbing your slumber if it wasn't a matter of urgency. Please join us on your free will. As I said, we are not asking as your alphas but as fellow warriors."

"Thank you for your time and answering our call."

As they spoke, I watched the orbs start to shimmer around. It was as if they were talking to each other. The orbs debated what was said to them in a light show that was spinning around the room.

"What is it that you need us to do?" a dark-blue orb said, moving out of the spinning tornado.

When he spoke though, the rest of the orbs stopped moving, the wind in the room came to a dead stop.

I stepped forward to answer the question. "Simply a distraction. The witches set fire to everything with lightning bolts from the skies. Burning the trees, fighting to kill all that stood. They fight as if they are controlled. Their blood is oil. Their eyes are gone. We aren't sure who's leading them because they are hiding in shadows. Anything you're willing and able to do, we will happily appreciate," I spoke, and it felt like hundreds of eyes were on me.

"Izzy?" came a cry from Tommy.

I looked over at him and saw him staring out the doorway. I turned to look where he was looking and had to move closer to the doorway to make sure I was seeing what I thought I was.

"Damien. They are here."

There were at least two witches standing on my porch, looking through the window with dead eyes. I felt movement behind me. Though I just knew it was the group of spirits that were now sorrowing me. Damien shifted and charged for the door. He took a witch down as another wolf flew over the fighting pair. I moved to the boys and herded them into the corning. Shaking out a folded blanket, I put it over their heads. Though I could hear Manny try to quiet Tommy who was terrified from what he saw standing out there. Spinning on my heel to face the room, I noticed all the orbs were shimmering again. Watching me closely, though, I wasn't sure what they were watching for.

"Zella! Grandma Zella, guide me."

"Child, send the trees and wake the forest. I got some tricks up these old shelves of mine. Don't you worry."

I had become so familiar with her blue orb that I could pick it out in a room full of energy balls floating over. Larger than I had ever seen, streaks of electricity were coming off it in waves. I moved out of the room and didn't look back. Moving out the door and off the porch, I wasn't looking around at the fighting around me. I just focused on the trees and skies. I knelt down and shoved my hands into the dirt to say the words needed to wake the lands.

Before I could get more than a sentence out though, a bolt of lightning landed just to my side barely missing me. I could feel the heat of it as it passed. That was when all hell broke loose. I could hear Zella's cry of rage then next thing I saw was all the orbs from that little room flying everywhere. It was like they tripled in numbers. They were zinging all over the lands and the trees. Looking up, I saw a witch go flying in the air and slammed into a tree. The ruthlessness that flew from the cabin was something that one day, if I lived through this, I would wonder over. The sight was almost gorgeous to see in their grace. War cries could be heard from all directions.

I braced myself into the ground again and got the chant out as fast as I could. Standing, I raised my hands to the sky to beg for the rains to put the fires out. I knew Zella had the power to do it, and though I never had tried it before, now seemed like a good time to see what gifts I got from her. Before I could finish though, another bolt of lightning came down. This time, it was a hit. I went soaring in the tree line only to have their leafy branches soften the impact.

I sat there slightly stunned, shaking my head to try and clear my brain. I looked off to the side to see the same branches that stopped my crash swing violently into the stomach of a witch. Roots were coming up from the ground as they moved, wreaking havoc. I started to crawl on my hands and knees back to the open grounds, feeling like my insides were on fire and not caring. Once I got under the clear night sky, I lifted my arms back up, straightening my back, and I started to chant until drops start to fall. Wolves were howling to the moon goddess as their snarling was getting louder. This was truly a battlefield of horror.

"Ms. Izzy!" I heard the scream and looked up to see Manny running off the porch straight into the fighting. He was running toward me with alligator tears streaming out of his eyes. "Izzy…"

I moved, getting to my feet. I charged for the boy only to see the witch come up from behind him with her hands stretched out as if to grab the boy. On instinct, I shifted in a run leap. I landed straight into the witch as we tumbled to the ground. She was oddly strong,

JORDAN BATT

and when we collided into the hard ground, she started to laugh like it was the time of her life. I fought like an angry mother wolf that needed to protect her pup. You never try and separate a mother from her pups. I clawed and snapped until the witch was no longer laughing. More lightning was falling all around us, though I didn't care as long as the threat to my boys was gone. Without thought, I kicked out my hind legs, knocking her into one of the bolts, and she fell to the ground.

I turned around looking for Manny only to see him crying harder. He looked scared out of his mind, and I shifted back into my human self. Manny ran straight for me and threw his arms around my neck.

"You need to get back into the cabin."

"No, you need me. You can't leave us too."

"I'm not going anywhere, I promise. Now we need to get back to the cabin." I couldn't carry him. For some reason, I couldn't seem to lift my arm, so I grabbed his hand and tried to run.

"Izzy," Manny cried out, and I looked behind me to see him.

Though I didn't see any threat coming right for us, I forced us to move forward. "We must get inside, honey. Everything will be fine."

But when I got to the steps, it was like all the power I had left my body, and I crashed; I fell down.

Manny put his arm around my back. "We're almost there, come on." He dragged me toward the door.

I lifted myself back up and staggered back in inside. The next thing I knew, I was in the safe room still not able to lift my arm. Though all three boys were safe and bundled around me, the sounds of the fight slowly became quieter as time faded on.

Once the sun started to rise and the howls of the wolves faded, rain started to pour down. That's when I knew it was over.

"Child. Child. Are you in here?" I heard Ms. Zella, but for the life of me, I couldn't answer her.

"In here. Zella, in here."

"Zella!" all the boys started to scream for her, and I looked up to see her bright light.

106

"Oh, dear. I must get Damien."

And just like that, the bright light started to fade away. The boys, though, they weren't crying. They just stayed there, lying around me. It was funny how fast these hoodlums grew on me. I couldn't imagine my life without them. My eyes were getting so tired. I was trying my best to keep them open, but they just kept drifting closed. At some point, the exhaustion must have won out because I drifted off.

CHAPTER 16

OPENING MY EYES, I looked around the room I was in and saw white walls around me. I wasn't in the hiding room anymore. Instead, I was in a hospital bed. Looking off to my left, I saw Damien sleeping in the chair with his head back. I heard something off to my side. Turning to look. I saw Bonnie coming into the room with her head down, flipping through papers on the clipboard.

"Whatcha looking at?"

"Izzy!" her screech echoed through the room, and Damien leaped out of his chair.

He was looking frantically to his left and right until the finally settled on me. "You're awake" was all he said as he sat back down in the chair.

"What happened?" I asked Bonnie as she came up next to me.

"To put it bluntly, you were hit with lightning."

"Yeah, I remember that part."

"Well, you see, umm, Izzy, I don't know how to say this."

"How about spitting it out, Bonnie. My head hurts. Let's just have it."

"Okay, fine. The lightning was magically generated and so we don't know how it will react completely. You're alive and healing. You've been asleep for three days and went through a fever. You will be okay though. Everything will be okay. We won though. The witches didn't last long after the rains started."

"Whatever you opened up in the sky came down like a monsoon. I have never seen anything like it." Damien had his elbows on his knees leaning forward.

"With that and the trees swinging in every direction, it was something unbelievable to watch. If I wasn't there, I wouldn't even believe it. The storm wiped up all the bolts of magic the witches were trying to throw. When those stopped, these balls of light came shooting out in all different directions. That reminds me... When you're feeling up for it, you have some visitors that want to see you."

"Visitors?"

"Yeah, as in a whole bunch of light things. Isabel, they talk and everything. One of them says that I'm his great-great-granddaughter? Do I want to know?"

"Well, you probably are his great-great-granddaughter, Bonnie. Those balls of lights are our ancestors from both the mountains and the flatlands. You remember Zella, right?"

"Of course and yes, I met her orb too. I screamed."

"That sounds about right." I started to laugh but stopped when it hurt my stomach. "She left me her books. It's a long story and I'll tell you later. Short story, Zella came back, and I found some of her old books. You know 'the books,' and I used them to make a call to somewhere. They came back to help us willingly. If it wasn't for them, there was no way we could have won. I promise I'll fill you in later. The orbs, though, are our friends."

"Yes, they have been very helpful. I thought the kids would be scared of them, but the orbs keep telling them stories. I think they are going to be the new pack tellers if they stay around."

"That's good. How's my father taking them?"

"Honestly, he's been really quiet since the fighting stopped," Bonnie said, looking down.

I was about to ask her what was wrong, but the soft knock on the door stopped anything I was going to say. I looked up to see Doc standing there holding two cups of coffee.

"You're up," he said, sounding greatly relieved. "Bonnie." He nodded at her very politely before making his way over to hand Damien a cup.

I couldn't help but notice that Bonnie stopped talking. Her whole demeanor changed the second he walked into the room. If I had to guess, I would say that she was angry, but I couldn't even guess what Doc could have done. He seemed nice enough to me. though I didn't really spend much time with him. Given the glare Bonnie had going on, I figured it would be good to give her a bit before asking her.

"How are you feeling, Isabel?" Doc asked me.

But before I could answer him, Bonnie yelled out the door causing the room to flood with orbs, "She's up!"

I couldn't even guess how many orbs were in the room, but they were all talking at once. I just laid my head back down and let them all go. They were so excited about the events that I couldn't help but smile. They must have lived very exciting lives once. Zella's light-blue orb settled down next to me on the bed.

It wasn't until Arthur spoke that the rest quieted down. "I think I know what changed the witches causing them to attack. Once there was this group of witches that thought they held the power to control the supernatural. They thought werewolves were meant to be like pets. As you can imagine, it didn't go over well with the wolves of the time. They practiced dark magic, though if I remember the stories correctly, they believed in a priestess of some kind," Arthur said.

"Why did they attack now though?"

"Because they wanted to try it again," Damien said.

"They wanted to see if the wolves have wreaked their bloodlines with breeding with humans," Arthur said.

There was no condemnation in his tone, though it sounded like he was just stating a fact.

"Mating with a human doesn't weaken the bloodline." This growl came from Henry.

The brothers' history was definitely coming to mind with this.

"I know, brother, it was a mistake, believe me, but it was one that was believed by more supernaturals than just me. Though the thought was wrong. I was wrong, brother. And it is something that I will forever be sorry for."

"It's all right. Time heals all, and besides, I've been stuck in a cave with you for centuries. We have gotten over this by now, didn't we?"

"Yes."

"Isabel." There was a voice at the door that made me want to pull the blanket over my head and pretend to not be here.

"Wayne," I growled in warning.

Beyond hurt, I didn't want him close to me, not after the crazy way he's been lately. Though before he could make his way into the room, Damien was up and rushed to the door. The orbs all parted like the sea to give him a path straight for him. All I saw was Damien tackling him around the waist and into the hall. The noise that was coming from the hallway left very little to the imagination about what was happening in the hallway. I couldn't believe Wayne was up in my hospital room. He was the last person I wanted to see.

CHAPTER 17

BEING BACK HOME WAS nice, and all I wanted to do was take a bath. Zella was floating about, talking to the brothers. A few of the orbs desired to stick around and learn about their great-great-grandchildren. When I was in the hospital, I got to meet some of them who stayed to join the fight. It was heartwarming to see that they all were so excited to see the children in their line. They wanted to be part of their lives. The ones who chose to go back to the moon goddess said their goodbyes and drifted away. I was truly happy that Zella chose to stay with me. I didn't think I would be able to say goodbye to her again. She was an amazing woman, and the children loved her being around.

The children were staying with Bonnie since I was hospitalized. From what I heard, the kids didn't want to leave the cabin, but the pack women wouldn't let them stay there alone. Apparently, Manny lost it when the women tried to take the boys out of the cabin. Little Tommy started to fight against them. All three of the boys came with me when Damien brought me to the hospital. Bonnie came out of surgery and calmed the boys down. She talked them into coming back to her apartment. Tommy's friend was released into her care as well, so the two boys were back together again. Personally, I liked the idea of the other boy joining the others. All those boys worked as a group, but I couldn't help but wonder how they were going to change.

Slowly moving through the halls to the bathroom, I started to run my tub. While the water was running, I went to the kitchen to start a cup of tea. Though my body was still sore, it was so nice to be home. There was something almost freeing about the relaxation that the room gave me. The witches were gone, the threat to the people was over, and the mountains were ours again. Though I couldn't help but feel the sadness like I lost something. Damien was going to go back home and so were the boys. Now that this was over, everything was going to go back to normal.

After the incident with Wayne at the hospital, I haven't seen him since. To my surprise, Stacy was at the hospital, and from what I heard, she wasn't too happy to find out what Wayne was doing there. I guess she didn't know that he was trying to talk me into being his mate. When Damien took him down is when she learned about it. The guys pulled Damien off of him only to have Stacy jump on him, slapping and yelling at him. From what I heard, Wayne ended up running away with his tail between his legs.

Getting into the bathroom with my cup of tea, I stripped down and sunk into the tub. I laid my head back and closed my eyes, drifting off into a light sleep until the water started to cool, which woke me. I finished washing up and eased my way out of the water. Wrapping a towel around me, I made my way out of the bathroom only to see Damien sitting there.

"Hey, what are you doing here?"

"Checking on you."

"Oh, well, I'm fine. I swear. Besides, it feels good to be clean and home."

"Speaking of home, I was wondering if you would want to come back up the mountain with me."

"What?"

"Do you want to live in the mountains? I want you to come with me."

I walked around the room, looking at everything around me but not really seeing any of it. I knew he was going to leave, but I didn't think he was going to want me to come with.

"I can't leave my cabin."

"I know I'm asking a lot, and we never talked about what was going to happen after all this was over with. Though I think you would really like it up there."

"I don't think I can just leave. This is my home."

"I know you've been through a lot, and I don't expect you to decide right now. Just think about it. Okay?"

"I need to. Well, I need to just rest for right now. This is a lot to take in at once."

"I understand. You rest. I'll be back later to check on you. I don't need an answer right away, just think about it." He kissed me on my cheek and turned to leave, moving up to the mountains.

I had never thought about moving away from here. To leave the cabin and Bonnie. These were the lands that I knew. I went over to sit on the couch only to have Zella come float next to me.

"Child. If it wasn't for your father, I would have moved away a long time ago. Damien isn't a bad guy."

"Do you think I should go?"

"Yes, I do. You only live once, Isabel, and Damien isn't a bad guy. If you stay here simply because of fear of new things, you're going to miss out on life. Besides, I'll be right there with you."

"You'll come with me?"

"Of course. You don't think you're going on an adventure without me, do you?"

"Well, of course not. Though how can we leave this place?"

"Sweetie, you need to follow your gut. What does it tell you to do?"

Before I could answer her, the door opened, and Bonnie walked in with all the boys in tow. She definitely seemed to have her hands full with them.

I opened my mouth and spoke without thought, "Bonnie, do you feel like a road trip?"

I told her about Damien's offer. The three of us sat at the table, discussing the options while the boys read in the other room. We talked until there was a knock on the back door. I got up to get it and was surprised that it was Damien. He never knocked, though this time, the imposing alpha looked anything but comfortable in his own skin.

He was standing there with flowers and a small smile. "Just checking back in to check on you."

"I'm fine. Do come in, won't you?" I moved out of his way, so he could enter the kitchen, though he paused when he saw Zella and Bonnie staring at him. "I thought about your offer, and I'll come with you on three conditions."

"And what are those?"

"One, Bonnie and Zella are coming with."

"Of course. Your friends and family are always welcome."

"Two, I can come and go as I please. I don't want to stay up there forever. I will come back down when I wish to."

"Again, understandable.

"Three, I want to take the cabin with me."

"You what?"

"The boys can stay with me if they wish, and I want to be responsible for their education and raising them. I want to take them in."

"That sounds perfect." He put his arms around me and hugged me tight, pulling back only to give me a kiss deep enough to make me melt into him.

In the background, I could hear Zella yelling, "Road trip!" and Bonnie was laughing. I could also hear the boys come into the room and give a collective "eww" at seeing us kissing. I broke away to turn and look at them smiling.

"What do you boys say? If I come to live up in the mountains, do you boys want to stay with me?"

The boys all nodded yes and then something in their eyes changed. It was a cheerful excitement.

"We can go back home."

"Yes."

"We start leaving in a week."

"A week? So soon."

"Well, some of us are leaving then to start rebuilding before everyone comes up. I leave in a week. You can come when you all are ready, though I do have to head over to the hall now. Some of the men here are going to help with the rebuilding part." He kissed my forehead and said his goodbyes to us for the night.

Zella was already bouncing in the air, yelling at us to come along to plan on how to start packing. This new chapter in my life was definitely going to be interesting. Though the fact that Zella and Bonnie were going to be coming with made it that much more exciting.

End.

ABOUT THE AUTHOR

Jordan grew up in Wisconsin where she was raised by her two parents as an only child. She was in special education for most of her schooling and lost her finger in a belt sander in sixth grade. With the love and support of her parents, she decided to follow her dreams and share her writing and imagination. She lives with her two cats, Slyvester and Carmella, and a dog, Crimson, that she spends most of her free time with. Her favorite hobbies are crocheting and playing a good game of cards.

Printed in the USA
CPSIA information can be obtained
at www.ICGtesting.com
LVHW052150070923
757597LV00029B/279